Dear Reader,

I can hardly believe that it is almost twenty years since I wrote my first Harlequin book. The thrill of having that book accepted and then seeing it on the bookshelves—being picked up and chosen by readers—is one I shall never forget.

Twenty years seems a long time. So much has happened during those years; so much has changed and yet so much remains the same. The changes that we have all seen within society are, I believe, reflected in the books we, as Harlequin authors, write. They mirror the changes that take place around us in our own and our readers' lives. Our heroines have changed, matured, grown up, as indeed I have done myself. I cannot tell you how much pleasure it gives me to be able to write of mature—as well as young—women finding love. And, of course, love is something that has not changed. Love is still love and always will be, because love is, after all, an intrinsic, vital component of human happiness.

As I read through these books that are being reissued in this Collector's Edition, they bring back for me many happy memories of the times when I wrote them, and I hope that my readers, too, will enjoy the same nostalgia and pleasure.

I wish you all very many hours of happy reading and lives blessed with love.

Penny Jordan

Back by Popular Demand

Penny Jordan is one of the world's best loved as well as bestselling authors, and she was first published by Harlequin in 1981. The novel that launched her career was *Falcon's Prey*, and since then she has gone on to write more than one hundred books. In this special collection, Harlequin is proud to bring back a selection of these highly sought after novels. With beautiful cover art created by artist Erica Just, this is a Collector's Edition to cherish.

Penny Jordan

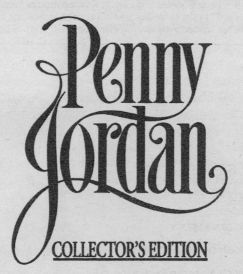

COLLECTOR'S EDITION

Passionate Relationship

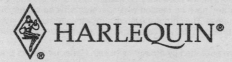

HARLEQUIN®

TORONTO • NEW YORK • LONDON
AMSTERDAM • PARIS • SYDNEY • HAMBURG
STOCKHOLM • ATHENS • TOKYO • MILAN • MADRID
PRAGUE • WARSAW • BUDAPEST • AUCKLAND

ISBN 0-373-83375-X

PASSIONATE RELATIONSHIP

First North American Publication 1987.

Copyright © 1987 by Penny Jordan.

ERICA JUST
cover illustrator for the
Penny Jordan Collector's Edition

Erica Just is an artist and illustrator working in various media, including watercolor, pen and ink, and textiles. Her studio is in Nottingham, England.

Her work is inspired by the natural forms, architecture and vibrant colors that she has experienced on her travels, most especially in Africa and India.

Erica has exhibited her work extensively in Great Britain and Europe and has works in private and public collections. As an illustrator she works for a number of companies and also lectures on textile design throughout the country.

CHAPTER ONE

ONLY another fifty kilometres or so to go. Shelley had paced herself and her ancient Citroën carefully during the long drive from London to Portugal, but now she was tempted to succumb to the long-suppressed sense of excitement fizzing inside her and put her foot down. But the deep vein of caution that life had bred in her stopped her.

With it came a wave of intense pain and sadness. If only she had made this journey six months ago. If only. . .

At twenty-four she considered herself long past such vain hopes, but it had been such a shock to discover the truth that in the last few days she had sometimes had difficulty recognising herself.

It was getting close to midday, the overhead August sun throwing sharp shadows across the dusty road as she drove through the centre of yet another sleepy village. Although she had often holidayed on the continent, this was her first visit to the Algarve, and it was not at all what she had expected. True, she was not driving along the coast, but she had not anticipated the degree of timelessness that embraced the land; she had driven past smallholdings of vines and fruit trees, tended by gnarled men and black-garbed women;

she had eaten in small dusty squares where the degree of courtesy and courtliness which had accompanied her sparse meals had entranced her.

The Algarve was a land that had once, long ago, known the beneficent and civilising hand of the Moors, a land from which had sprung a race of seagoing adventurers who had carved out for themselves an empire.

Thinking about what she had read about the country helped to quell the nervous butterflies fluttering in her stomach. Nervous? Her? Shelley grimaced faintly to herself, well aware how surprised and even disbelieving her colleagues would be if they could see into her mind now.

She knew that at work she had the reputation of being cool and very, very controlled. Too controlled and withdrawn, in some people's eyes. She had once been told by one of her university professors that she was far too wary of human contact, too determined to keep her guard up, and she knew that it was true. After getting her degree she had deliberately chosen a large organisation over a small company, wanting the anonymity such an organisation would give her, needing it to preserve her defence systems.

She had risen quickly from her first position and was now head of the department responsible for all the company's overseas contracts. She had flown on company business to Australia and the States, and even to the Far East, but none of those journeys had given her one tenth of the sense of excitement and fear she was experiencing now.

But then this journey was different. It was a journey into her past, a journey to meet the family she had never even known she possessed until four weeks ago.

Even now, Shelley could scarcely credit the fragile chain of coincidences that had brought her on this journey. If she had not refused a date with Warren Fielding, and decided to spend her Sunday in the reading room of a local museum, she would never have seen the advertisement, never have known the truth.

Several men had shown an interest in her over the years, although she couldn't understand why. Lacking in self-confidence, she could see nothing particularly attractive in the way she looked. She was just above medium height, with shiny, thick brown hair enlivened with copper highlights. Her skin, like her hair, betrayed traces of her Celtic origins, being fair and flawlessly clear. Her eyes were almond-shaped and could change from gold to green depending on her mood.

Since she had known almost as soon as she was able to understand the spoken word that no man would ever want to marry her, she had never been burdened with the need to impress any member of the male sex, and so she chose her clothes and make-up according to her own tastes rather than theirs. Additionally, her crisp, cool manner was one that suited *her*, rather than being designed to flatter and attract.

Irrationally, or so it seemed to Shelley, some men seemed to find her very indifference a challenge. Warren Fielding had been the most persistent of this breed. An American colleague, he made a point of getting in touch with her every time he came to London, and Shelley had discovered that her best defence against his invitations was simply not to be at home to answer her phone.

Her circle of friends was very small, mainly composed of girls she had been at Oxford with, now all married or working abroad, and hence her Sunday visit to the museum reading room.

What whim had compelled her to start reading the personal columns of the newspaper, she did not really know, but the shock that gripped her when her own name leaped off the page at her was something she would never forget. She had read the advertisement over and over again, wondering why on earth any firm of solicitors, but especially one with such an establishment-sounding name as Macbeth, Rainer & Buccleugh, should want her to get in touch with them.

She had waited until the Wednesday of the following week before telephoning the London number, reluctant to admit to her own curiosity. An appointment had been made for that afternoon, and contrary to her expectations she had discovered that Charles Buccleugh was relatively young; somewhere around the forty mark, with a charming smile and a desk full of framed photographs of his family.

When he mentioned the name of her father her first instinct had been to get up and walk out.

Only her self-control stopped her. She had taught herself years ago that it was a hard fact of life that there were countless thousands of children in the same position as herself: unwanted by the men who had fathered them.

It had been from her grandmother that she had learned the sad but common story of her parents' marriage. Her mother had married against parental advice, and it was no surprise that the marriage had ended as it had, her grandmother had constantly told her. The moment he knew his wife was pregnant, her father had started to neglect the young girl he had married. 'He disappeared for weeks at a time—told your mother he was looking for a job. But I knew better. I told your grandfather how it would be from the moment she met him. Thank the Lord he didn't live long enough to see how right I was.'

Shelley knew that her grandfather had died before she was born. She also knew from her grandmother that shortly before she was born, her father had deserted her mother, leaving her alone at nineteen with no one to turn to apart from her mother.

'Of course, they had been living with us right from the start of the marriage. I insisted on that,' she had been told. 'I wasn't going to allow my daughter to be dragged off to some dirty one-room flatlet. She could have done so well for herself, too. All he was interested in was his drawing. Never even tried to get himself a decent job. Your grandfather and I never approved. Of course, your poor mother was heartbroken when he left, but I'd warned her all along how it would be. Six weeks and he was gone, without so much as a word. You were born prematurely, and my poor Sylvia died almost before you drew a single breath. Four weeks later we heard that your father had been killed in a road accident. Good riddance, I thought.'

Here her grandmother's mouth would always tighten, and she would warn Shelley against giving her heart to any man.

'In my day we had to marry,' she would tell her granddaughter, 'but for you it's different. You have a choice. I don't want the same thing that happened to your mother to happen to you.'

Gradually, as she grew up, Shelley had learned that her grandparents' marriage had not been a happy one. There had been a long-standing affair between her grandfather and someone else in the early part of their marriage, which seemed to have soured the relationship. Her grandmother didn't like the male sex, and she had brought Shelley up to feel the same way. As a young child she had felt the pain of her mother's loss and betrayal as though it had been her own, her vivid imagination all too easily able to conceive the anguish her young mother must have known. And now she was being told that her father wasn't dead at all, and that moreover, for the last eight years he had been searching desperately for her.

The story Charles Buccleugh revealed to her was almost too astonishing to be true. It appeared that, contrary to what her grandmother had told her, her father's search for work had been genuine, and that, moreover, he had actually found a job in London. He had written to her mother, giving her the good news, and telling her that he would be coming home to collect her.

It was during that journey that he had been involved in the accident that her grandmother had claimed ended his life. He had been injured, quite badly, so badly that the hospital authorities hadn't realised he was married until he himself was able to tell them.

Immediately they helped him to write a letter to her mother, telling her what had happened, but the reply he received to it came from her grandmother, informing him that both his wife and child were dead.

He had been too ill to leave the hospital to make the journey home, and a week later he had received another letter from his mother-in-law, advising him that the funerals had taken place and that she never wanted to see him again.

Stricken with grief himself, he could well appreciate that she must blame him for the tragedy, and gradually he had started to rebuild his own life. He had always wanted to be an artist, and with the compensation money he received for the accident he had gone out to Portugal to paint.

Several years later he had remarried—a widow with two children of her own, and then by the most amazing of coincidences he had bumped into an old acquaintance from his home town, who was holidaying on the Algarve with his family. It was from him that he learned that he had a daughter, but by that time her grandmother was dead, and Shelley had gone through a series of foster parents, and despite all his efforts he had been unable to trace her.

Now he was dead, and apparently it had been his dearest wish that somehow his lost daughter was found, hence the advertisement in the paper.

'There is a bequest to you in his will,' Charles Buccleugh had told her, 'but you'll have to get in touch with his Portuguese solicitors to find out about that. We're only acting on their instructions to find you, or rather on the instructions of his stepson, the Conde Jaime y Felipe des Hilvares.'

Shelley had raised her eyebrows a little at the title, although she permitted herself to show no great degree of surprise or shock. Under the calm exterior she was showing the solicitor, she was still trying to come to terms with the fact that her grandmother had deliberately withheld the truth from her. She had long ago come to recognise that fact that her grandmother disliked the male sex, but to discover that she had deliberately lied to her about her father's death was something Shelley was finding it very hard to accept.

All those wasted years. . .

She said the words out loud without being aware that she had done so as she drove through yet another dusty village. In front of her the road forked, one fork ribboning down towards the coast and the sea she could see glittering under the hot sun, the other reaching higher into the hills.

This was the fork she had to take. It would lead her eventually to the home of the Conde, and presumably the rest of his family. Her family. . .

All those years when she had ached for a family of her own, a real family, believing she ached for the impossible, when all the time. . . A different woman would have wept for all that might have been, but that was not Shelley's way.

As a young child she had been too acutely aware of the fact that in her grandmother's eyes she was somehow tainted with the blood of her father, and had learned young to hide her feelings and her pain. What she felt now was beyond relief in easy tears. It was too anguished, too tormented with all that might have been.

All those years when she might have known her father and had not. She wasn't really interested in whatever it was he had left her in his will; that wasn't what brought her to Portugal. No, what she had come for was to learn about the man who had been her father.

Had he too known this aching anguish that now possessed her? This mingling of bitter resentment and helpless compassion for the woman who had so deliberately kept them apart?

A signpost warned her that she must turn off for her destination, the road running between rows of well-tended vines. Her stepbrother was a wine producer, or so Charles Buccleugh had told her. This could well be his land. Was he, she wondered, as regimented and formal as his vines?

All she knew about her father's second family was that his stepson was older than she was and his stepdaughter younger. It had been a surprise to discover that her stepmother was half English. What sort of woman would be attracted to a Portuguese *conde* and a penniless English artist? An unpleasant thought struck her. Could her father have married for money?

She shivered slightly, pushing the thought away. Hadn't she already decided that it was foolish to prejudge the situation? She knew nothing about her step-family or the life her father had lived here in Portugal apart from the fact that he had continued to paint. Charles Buccleugh had known that much at least. Indeed, he had seemed almost amused by her own tentative questioning on this point, although she didn't know why.

It had been the Portuguese solicitors in Lisbon who had informed her that her stepbrother wished her to travel to his home. Although his request had seemed a little high-handed, she had been due some leave, and there was no reason why, if she found her step-family in the slightest degree uncongenial, she should not simply get into her car and drive home.

The mingling of anticipation and dread she was experiencing was an unfamiliar sensation. She didn't normally allow herself to be so troubled by 'nerves', but for once her notorious self-control seemed to be deserting her.

The road crested a small hill, and she caught her breath in shocked delight as she had her first glimpse of her destination.

Below her, nestling in the curve of the hills, lay a collection of buildings whose whitewashed walls and terracotta tiled roofs should have looked untidy, but instead looked entrancingly picturesque. So much so, in fact, that Shelley found herself having to blink to make sure she was not daydreaming.

The lines of vines ran straight and true right up to the wall which surrounded the house and gardens, and although it was impossible for her to hear such a sound from so far away, she could almost have sworn she heard the sound of water falling from fountains. In her mind's eye already she could almost see the interlocking paved court-yards that were so much a feature of Moorish buildings; she could almost smell the pungent aroma of coffee and taste the sticky sweetness of the little cakes so beloved of these people of the south.

Indeed the scene below her was so familiar she could not believe she had never actually beheld it before. Telling herself she was being over-imaginative, she found her handbag and checked that her hair and makeup looked neat and fresh.

The face that stared back at her from the small mirror was reassuringly familiar, her expression faintly aloof and withdrawn, the cleverly tailored cut of her thick glossy hair making it fall in a smooth, controlled curve.

It was only natural that her heart should start to pound so suffocatingly fast as she re-started the car, but because she was so unused to these nervous tremors their effect on her was magnified, causing her to grip the steering wheel tightly.

A narrow road, dusty and uneven, led down to her destination. The white wall surrounding the buildings was higher than she had anticipated, throwing out a dark shadow. The two wooden doors that guarded the arched entrance stood open, and as she drove in underneath it Shelley heard, quite unmistakably, the sound of fountains. So she had been right about those at least!

Seen at closer quarters, the house was larger than she had thought: two-storied and very rambling. Somewhere inside the building a dog barked, but apart from that, no sound disturbed the hot silence of the afternoon.

She had, she realised, arrived at the time of siesta. Without the engine running, the interior of her small car was quickly becoming stifling. Opening the door, she gazed at the heavily studded arched doorway in front of her. In style it mirrored the one through which she had just driven, and she suspected that it must lead into one of the secret interior courtyards so beloved by people of Moorish descent.

Climbing stiffly out of the car, she was halfway towards the door when the clatter of a horse's hoofs attracted her attention.

The sun was in her eyes as she turned to look

at the horse and rider. She had a confused impression of a tall, dark-haired man seated astride an equally large and dark horse before the sharp glitter of the sun made her close her eyes and man and horse merged into the shadows.

Fumbling for her sunglasses, she put them on, and looked up at the rider.

'Miss Howard, I presume.'

Whoever he was he spoke perfect English, even if his voice did hold a tinge of sarcastic contempt.

Never one to let a challenge slip by uncontested, Shelley raised her head and, using her coolest voice, agreed silkily, 'Yes, I am she. And you, *senhor*. . .?'

'Your stepbrother, Jaime y Felipe des Hilvares—but you must call me Jaime.' As he spoke he swung down from his horse, and from round the side of the building a gnarled, bow-legged man came hurrying to take the reins from him and lead the animal away.

Her new stepbrother said something to the groom in Portuguese, the language making his voice far softer and more liquid than it had appeared when he spoke to her. The groom's face split in a wide smile, his head nodding. '*Sim, Excelentíssimo. . . sim. . .*'

Against her will Shelley suffered a sharp sense of shock. She had known of course about her stepbrother's title, but such a blatant acknowledgement of it was not something she had anticipated.

He looked arrogant, she thought, studying him covertly and trying to quell her sense of suddenly having stepped on to very unfamiliar and alien ground. There was nothing in her background or her present life to equate with this. Contrarily, she decided she was not going to let that put her at a disadvantage. If her stepbrother chose to be supercilious and contemptuous towards her because he possessed a title and she did not, well, he would soon learn that she was not so easily cowed.

'It is rather hot out here, Jaime,' she said, 'and I have had a long drive. . .'

'Indeed. . .and yet you look remarkably cool and fresh.'

He was looking at her assessingly, hard grey eyes studying her slender form in its covering of white top and jeans.

'We are very honoured that you have at last chosen to visit us, and you do right to remind me that I am being less than courteous in keeping you standing here in our hot sun. Please follow me.'

Again his voice was tinged with sarcasm, his mouth hardening imperceptibly as he moved towards her, his whole manner towards her somehow suggesting that he was holding himself tightly in control, and that beneath that cool polite surface simmered a dislike he was only just holding in check.

But why should he dislike her?

He moved, the sunlight shining sharply across

his face, revealing for the first time the high
cheekbones and harshly carved features that were
another legacy of the Moors' occupation of the
Algarve. His skin was tanned a warm gold,
making her all too aware of her own pallor. Her
skin was very pale and only coloured very slowly.
She felt positively anaemic standing at the side
of this dark-haired, golden-skinned man. She also
felt almost frighteningly small and fragile. She
had not expected him to be so tall, easily six foot
with the broad shoulders and muscled body of
an experienced rider. As he walked towards the
door, Shelley saw that he moved with a
coordinated litheness that was curiously pleasing
to the eye.

'I thought you wanted to go inside because
you were too hot?' He was watching her she saw,
his expression politely aloof, but his mouth gave
him away. It was curled in open, contemptuous
dislike. The shock of that dislike drove away her
embarrassment at being caught scrutinising him.

His aloofness she could have accepted, even
approved of; after all, it was her own response
to strangers and acquaintances. But his contempt!
The contempt of her peers was something she
had never had to deal with. On the contrary, she
was aware that most people who knew her held
her faintly in awe and accorded her their respect.
In her work she had occasionally come across
men who affected to despise the female species
in its entirety, but her crisp no-nonsense manner
soon convinced them that she was not going to

be influenced by such anti-female tactics. And anyway, Jaime was not anti-women, not trying to prove some superior male psychology. It was *her* he despised. She had seen that plainly enough in his eyes. But why?

Warily she followed him into the cool tiled hall. The shutters had been closed to keep out the strong heat of the sun and, momentarily blinded, she missed her step and grabbed instinctively at his arm.

Beneath his shirt sleeve his muscle were hard and rigid, his flesh warm and dry. Her fingertips seemed acutely sensitive all of a sudden, relaying to her his abhorrence of her touch. Even so, he courteously helped her regain her balance.

Perhaps it was the way she looked that he didn't like, Shelley pondered as her eyes adjusted to the dim light. Perhaps. . . Abruptly she curtailed her thoughts. What did it matter why he didn't like her? She had come here for one purpose, and that was to discover the father she had never known she had. Her inheritance from him, whatever it might be, was of secondary and very little importance. She had no assets in the sense that her stepbrother would consider such matters, but she had a well-paid job and had supported herself virtually from the moment she went to Oxford. She liked and felt proud of her financial independence, and whatever her father left would be cherished because he had been the donor, because he had after all cared about her and loved her, rather than for its monetary value.

Several doors gave off the hallway. As he showed her into one of them, Jaime explained that the main part of the house was built round an open courtyard and that most of the rooms overlooked this cool oasis.

'Through the years more rooms and smaller courtyards have been built on to suit the family's needs. In Portugal it is the custom for several generations to share a home. This house passed to me from my father when I attained my majority, but naturally my mother and sister make their home with me.'

'And my father. . .'

There was a small pause and then he said coolly,

'He too lived here sometimes, although he had preferred his own house, which is on the coast.'

The note of restraint in his voice made Shelley frown. 'This house. . .'

'I appreciate how anxious you are to discover your father's financial standing, Miss Howard,' Jaime broke in harshly, making it plain that although he had given her permission to use his first name he preferred to maintain a cool distance between them by not using hers. 'But these matters are best discussed with the *advogado* in Lisbon. I have arranged that he will call here tomorrow to discuss with you all the matters appertaining your father's will—and now, if you will excuse me, I will get one of the maids to show you to your room. She will bring you some refreshment. We dine earlier here than in Spain, normally about eight in the evening. Again, Luisa will tell you.'

Already he was turning away from her, and incredibly, Shelley realised he intended to walk out and leave her.

Anger battled with trepidation. It was galling to discover how little she wanted to be left alone in this alien environment, no matter how attractive it might be, and no matter how unwelcoming her host.

'Your mother and sister. . .'

'They are out shopping at the moment, but will return in time for dinner.'

He saw her face and smiled cruelly. 'What is wrong? Surely you cannot have expected to be greeted with a fatted calf? I must say that I admire your. . .courage, Miss Howard. It is not every child who would only condescend to visit the home of its father in such a blatant quest for financial gain. When I think of his attempts to contact you. . .his grief. . .' He swallowed hard, and over and above her shock at his obvious misconception of her motives, once again Shelley had the impression of intense anger being held tautly in control. 'No, you are not welcome in my home,' he continued, 'and nor shall I pretend that you are. For the love and respect I had for your father I am willing to see that his wishes are carried out. My mother is not here to greet you because she is still suffering desperately from her loss. Your father was the most important person in her life. Why didn't you come before. . .while he was still alive? Or was it your inheritance that drew you here and not the man?'

He threw the question at her harshly, but she was too shocked to formulate an answer. Turning on his heel, he left the room abruptly.

Standing in the shadows, Shelley shivered. So now she knew the reason for his contempt. He thought. . . She took a deep, steadying breath, wondering if she could call him back and tell him the truth, but somehow it seemed to be too much effort. Incredibly, she felt as weak and shaky as though she had just gone through an intense physical and emotional ordeal. She felt almost bruised both inwardly and outwardly.

She would have given anything to drive away from the *quinta* and never return, but she owed it to her father's memory to stay. Seen from her stepbrother's viewpoint, perhaps he and his family had good reason to think the way they did, but surely they might have given her the benefit of the doubt; might have waited, and not pre-judged. The stubborn pride she had inherited from her grandmother urged her to leave now and ignore her father's bequest, but she had come too far, gone through too much to leave now without accomplishing her mission.

She had come to Portugal with a purpose, and that purpose was to learn about the father that she had not known she had until recently; she was not going to allow her arrogant, judgemental stepbrother or his family to stop her. They could think what they liked of her, but she intended to make it clear to them that it wasn't avarice that had brought her to their home, unless a desire to learn about the man who had been her father could be classified as a form of greed.

So silently that she almost made her jump, a young girl came into the room.

'I am Luisa,' she informed Shelley with a charming accent. 'I show you to your room, *sim*. . . Yes?'

'Yes, please.'

CHAPTER TWO

BY accident rather than design, Shelley didn't make it to the dinner table at eight o'clock. Instead, it was gone ten when she finally surfaced from a deep but unrestful sleep. The brief span of time it took for her to recognise her surroundings was accompanied by a downward lurch of her stomach and a sense of growing despondency.

She had come to Portugal with such high hopes, and foolishly romantic ones, she realised now, ruthlessly exposing to her own self-criticism the folly of her ridiculous longings for a family of her own—the sort of family that comprised brothers and sisters, aunts, uncles and cousins, the sort of family she had heard colleagues bemoan times without number, the sort of family, she had told herself staunchly when her grandmother died, that she did not need.

Dreams took a long time to die, she recognised emptily, but last night hers finally had. She was not welcome here in Portugal. Even once the misconceptions surrounding her reasons for coming to Portugal were sorted out, she would still not be welcome. Her pride demanded that she didn't leave the *quinta* until she had made it plain to Jaime exactly why she had come, but her pride also demanded that no matter what

27

apology he might make, no matter how he might
seek to make amends for misjudging her, she
would hold him at a distance.

He wasn't what she had wanted in a stepbrother anyway. It was impossible for her to ever
envisage him in a brotherly role. That overwhelming aura of sexual magnetism of his would
always be something she was far too much aware
of. She shivered a little, goosebumps forming on
her flesh as she remembered the contemptuous
way he had looked at her.

Outside her open window she could hear the
sound of crickets, the warm air stirring the cur-
tains, reminding her that she was now in a foreign
country.

She felt thirsty, and far too keyed up to go
back to sleep. Her cases were neatly stacked on
a long, low chest; someone had emptied them
while she slept. Opening the wardrobe, she took
out a slim-fitting cotton dress.

She managed to find her way to the top of the
stairs without difficulty, but once down in the
hall was totally confused as to the whereabouts
of the kitchen. Her throat, which had felt merely
slightly dry when she first woke up, now felt like
sandpaper and, calculating back how long it had
been since she had last had a drink, she suspected
she might be suffering slightly from dehydration.

She felt more vulnerable and unsure of herself
than she could remember feeling for a long time.
The years in foster homes had taught her well
how to guard herself against the hurts unwittingly

inflicted by others. It had been a long time since anyone had been allowed to hurt her, and even longer since she had cried, but today she had come perilously close to experiencing both.

The sharp sound of a door opening made her jump, her face setting in lines of cold rejection as she saw her host striding towards her.

'So, you have decided to grace us with your presence after all. A pity you did not deign to join us for dinner.'

The insolent contempt in his voice banished all her good intentions not to let him provoke her into further hostilities. Acting with an impulsiveness that later would shock her, Shelley responded curtly. 'Why should I? You obviously know exactly what I'm here for, so, as you've already made abundantly plain, there is scarcely any need for the normal civilities between us.'

She saw that something in her cold words had caught him on a sensitive spot. A wave of dark colour—probably anger rather than embarrassment—stained the tanned skin, his eyes glittering with suppressed rage. She had once read somewhere that these Moorish Portuguese were a very proud and correct race, and she judged that he would not appreciate her criticism of his reception of her.

Spurred on by her success, she added dulcetly, 'You're obviously a very clever man, Jaime, to be able to analyse so correctly and assess the reactions of others without meeting or knowing them.'

This time he had himself well under control, only his voice faintly clipped and harsh as he responded, 'You flatter me, I'm afraid. In your case very little intelligence was needed; one merely had to look at the facts. A daughter who refuses to make herself known to her father until after his death, when almost miraculously she suddenly appears on learning that he had left her something of value; who would not even have given herself the trouble of coming out here at all if I hadn't insisted that she did. Why did you never make any attempt to trace your father? While you were a child I can see that you must have felt bound by your grandmother's desire not to see him, but once she had died—and I understand from the enquiries instituted by the lawyers that she died when you were fourteen— surely then you must have felt some curiosity about your father, some desire to find him?'

Her heart was pounding so heavily she could hardly breathe. It was plain to Shelley that Jaime had no idea to the real truth: that her grandmother had brought her up in the belief that her father was dead. But the same stubborn pride that had helped her endure so much as a child now refused to allow her to ask this man for his understanding or pity.

Instead of telling him the truth, she said curtly, 'Must I?'

The absolute contempt in his eyes fuelled her anger, pushing her through the barrier of logic and caution to the point where she heard herself saying huskily, in a voice vibrating with emotion, 'And by what absolute right do you dare to criticise me? You know nothing, either about me or about my motives in coming here. You are unbelievable, do you know that? You have the arrogance to criticise and condemn me without even trying to discover the facts; without knowing the first thing about me!' Her eyes flashed huge and dark in her too-pale face, the violence of her emotions draining her last reserves of energy. She was literally shaking with the force of them, knowing that she was no match either physically or emotionally for this man, but driven to defy him.

'I'm not staying here another minute!' her voice rising now, her strength rushing away from her. 'I'm leaving—right now.'

She turned sharply on her heel, her thirst forgotten, her one desire to leave the *quinta* just as soon as she could, but her flight was arrested by the hard fingers gripping her arm.

'Be still!'

The rough shake that accompanied the hissed words almost rattled her teeth. She turned to look at him with loathing, shocked into immobility as the door he had come through suddenly opened and a woman stood there.

'Jaime, *querido*, what is going on?'

She spoke in English, but even without that, Shelley would have know that this fair-haired woman could not be Portuguese.

So this was her father's wife. . .her stepmother.

As she looked into the delicately boned, fragile face, Shelley recognised the grief and pain in it. Yes, this woman had loved her father. A lump of cold ice formed round her own heart, the pain she had suffered as a child gripping her in a death hold as she met the worried blue eyes that looked first at her and then at Jaime.

'Miss Howard seems to want to leave us,' Jaime told his mother curtly. 'I am just about to impress upon her the inadvisability of such a course of action. For one thing the village has no guest house or hotel, and for another, the *advogado* arrives tomorrow morning to discuss with her those matters relating to her father's estate which concern her.'

Now, for the first time, her stepmother was forced to look at her. Up until now she had been avoiding doing so, Shelley recognised bleakly.

'So you are Philip's daughter. Your father. . .' Tears welled in her eyes and she turned her head away. Jaime released Shelley's arm to go to his mother's side, his obvious care and concern for her so much in contrast to the way he had spoken to and touched Shelley that she felt her resentment and misery increase.

Part of her longed to burst out that it wasn't fair, that she hadn't been responsible for the split with her father, that she had suffered too, but caution and pain tied her tongue. She was not going to reveal her vulnerability in front of this man. He would enjoy seeing her pain. . . Oh, he would cloak his enjoyment with a polite semblance of concern, but deep down inside he would enjoy it.

The door opened again and a young girl came out. In her stepsister the Portuguese strain was less obvious than it was in Jaime, but she had her brother's dark hair and olive skin.

Jaime said something to her in Portuguese, and after flicking a brief glance at Shelley she gently led her mother away.

'I strongly advise you against leaving here tonight,' Jaime told her coldly when his mother and sister had gone. 'Of course, if you insist then I cannot stop you, but as I mentioned earlier, the *advogado* arrives tomorrow morning; there will be much he will want to discuss with you.'

'And a great deal I shall want to discuss with him,' Shelley told him fiercely. 'Very well, *Excelentíssimo*.' She let the title roll off her tongue with bitter sarcasm. 'I shall stay until I have seen him, but believe me, your hospitality is as unwelcomely accepted by me as it is given by you.'

Before he could say another word she turned on her heel and went back upstairs. She was still thirsty, but she was damned if she would ask him for as much as a glass of water. God, how she hated him! When she got into her room she found that her nails had dug so deeply into her palms that they had left tiny crescent-shaped marks.

She was just on the point of getting back into bed when she heard a brief knock on the door. Stiffening slightly, she stared as it opened inwards.

The sight of her stepbrother carrying a tray of tea and sandwiches was the last thing she had expected. Her eyes rounded hugely as he carried it over to the bed and put it down beside her.

As though he sensed her shock he drawled mockingly, 'You might be unwelcome among us, but it is not our policy to starve our guests.'

Her mouth almost watered at the thought of a cup of tea, but a coldly gracious, 'Thank you,' was the only acknowledgement of his thoughtfulness that she made. In truth, she was too shocked to say anything else. That he should actually think to provide her with something to eat and drink after the row they had just had totally astounded her, but then perhaps his Latin temperament was more accustomed to such heated exchanges than hers. And yet he had not struck her as a temperamental person; far from it. She had received an initial impression of a very cool and controlled man indeed.

'My mother asks you to forgive her for not greeting you personally, but, as you will have seen, she is still suffering from the effects of your father's death.'

'Unlike me, you mean?'

The hostility was there again, his eyes burning their message of bitter contempt into hers as he leaned towards her, palms flat against her mattress.

'You said it, not I,' he told her coldly. 'But since you have said it, you leave me free to comment that I do find your very obvious lack of grief rather. . .disturbing.'

Shelley could have told him that she had cried many tears for her father over the years, and more since learning the truth, but her grief was a very private thing, not something she could easily find relief for. She could have told him that, unlike his mother, she had no one to turn to, no shoulder to cry on, no firm supporting male arm to comfort her. Instead she said mockingly, 'I'm surprised to learn that anything or anyone can disturb you, Jaime, least of all someone as insignificant and unworthy as myself.'

'Unworthy, maybe, but insignificant, never.'

Shelley caught her breath as her heartbeat suddenly accelerated wildly. He was insinuating that he found her sexually desirable—but surely that was impossible? For no reason at all she felt acutely conscious of the fact that she was in bed and wearing her nightdress, even if it was a very sensible cotton affair without the slightest pretensions to being provocative. For one inexplicable and totally appalling moment she found herself wondering what it would be like to be held in those sinewy male arms, to feel that cynical, masculine mouth caressing her own. The treacherous direction of her thoughts shocked her into tensing back, her eyes widening with shock.

Appallingly, as though his mind too had travelled along the same intimate lines, Jaime raised one hand and touched her face. The sensation of the hard pads of his fingertips against her skin

made her jerk back in horror, her reaction registered by the hard gleam in his eyes.

'Unpleasant, isn't it?' he agreed softly. 'But
then nature does so enjoy playing these little
tricks on us. For all that I, in my role as your
father's stepson, despise and dislike you, as a
daughter, as a man I cannot avoid knowing that
I would very much like to discover if all that fire
and temper you have inside you would be there
if we were together in bed. Lust is a tremendous
leveller, but you need not worry; for both our
sakes I intend to make sure that neither of us
gives in to such an unseemly desire.'

Did he really desire her, or was he just trying
to intimidate her? Surely it must be the latter?

Wordlessly Shelley watched as he got up and
walked to the door. There were a *thousand* things
she should have said to him, the most important
of which was an instant denial that she felt the
slightest degree of desire for him, but inexplic-
ably she had said nothing.

It was no wonder she hadn't slept well, Shelley
reflected tiredly, studying her reflection rather
grimly, and wondering what she should wear for
this morning's meeting with the *advogado*.
Something cool, and yet not too casual; clothes
were important. As she had quickly learned in
her business life, it was impossible to be judged
quite erroneously, simply on the manner of one's
dress. At home she would have had no problems.
One of the elegant tailored outfits she wore for

work would have done admirably, but she had not brought them with her.

Now that she had met her formidable stepbrother, she could see that that had been a mistake. Had he met her when she was dressed in her businesslike grey pinstripe suit instead of in casual jeans and top, he would not have dared to talk so insultingly about wanting to go to bed with her.

The hand applying her eyeshadow wavered slightly, and she cursed under her breath. With the morning had come a return of her normal self-control. Indeed, she found it hard to accept her own emotional outburst of the previous evening. Obviously it had been brought on by tiredness and shock. With hindsight she could see that it had been on the cards that her father's second family would resent her. When Jaime accused her of being motivated by greed he was no doubt unaware that his erroneous assessment of her gave her the suspicion that his own motives might not be completely untainted by that same vice.

It stood to reason that for her father to leave her something must mean that that same something couldn't be left to any members of his new family, and yet surely, with all the wealth so obviously possessed by Jaime and his family, they could hardly resent whatever small trifle of remembrance her father might want to leave her?

But then the rich were notorious for their meanness. As for Jaime saying he desired her. . .

Her hand shook again, and she steadied it, frowning fiercely at her own reflection. No doubt that had simply been something he had thrown at her to disarm her. A man with his brand of sexuality and good looks could scarcely be unaware of his effect upon her sex. No doubt it amused him to pretend some fictitious feeling of desire for her.

Did he think her so stupid that she was not aware of his contempt, or of the fact that even if he did genuinely desire her, his own pride would ensure that that desire was quite ruthlessly stifled?

A knock on her door made her jump, but it was only the maid, who had come to collect her breakfast tray.

'The Conde asks me to say to you that Senhor Armandes will be here in half an hour.'

Shelley waited until she had gone to continue her toilet. Her bedroom had two large windows, one overlooking the vine covered hillsides and the other, a large enclosed courtyard. She could have had her breakfast on the balcony that overlooked this courtyard, but she had purposely stayed in her room. She had no wish to look down from her balcony and find herself under observation by her stepbrother, and one quick look into the courtyard earlier on had shown her a table set for breakfast.

Stoically, she had refused to allow herself to be hurt by the fact that she had not been invited to join the family for breakfast. They did not want to welcome her among them; very well, that

would be their loss and not hers. She had no
real need of them, and if they chose to leap to
completely unfounded conclusions about the fact
that she had not made contact with her father
before his death, well then, let them.

Her watch told her that she had still fifteen
minutes to wait until the *advogado* arrived, and
she was determined not to set foot out of her
room until he did. Once she had spoken to him
she intended to leave the *quinta* just as quickly
as she could. Her bags were already packed.
Unable to sleep, she had risen early before Luisa
arrived with her tray and had soon packed away
everything that the maid had so carefully hung
up the evening before.

It was pointless regretting the lack of the chilly
formality of her business outfits, but she had had
the forethought to bring a tailored linen suit with
her, and she put this on now, frowning a little
over the soft mint green colour, unaware of how
poignantly the easy fit of the skirt showed up her
recent weight loss.

Make-up was a wonderful disguise, she
decided grimly, glancing at her watch and carefully removing the last of her personal belongings
from the room.

Calculating how much petrol she had left in
her car and how far it was to the last garage she
had passed on her drive occupied the last few
minutes before she heard a polite knock on
her door.

'The *advogado* is here,' Luisa told her shyly when she opened it.

She could see the maid glancing past her, her eyes widening as she saw the suitcases on the bed.

'I shall be leaving shortly, Luisa,' said Shelley coolly. 'Thank you for looking after me so well.'

She suspected it would be considered bad form for her to offer the girl a tip, but she had bought herself a new bottle of perfume before leaving home and luckily it was unopened. She would leave it as a present for the girl, whose open-mouthed surprise betrayed that she had expected Shelley's visit to be of a much longer duration.

'If you will just direct me. . .'

Collecting herself, the girl said hurriedly, 'The *advogado* is in the Conde's study. I will show you the way.'

As she followed the maid Shelley realised that there must be more than one flight of stairs to the ground floor of the house, and then wondered if it had been built along the Moorish lines of separate wings for various members of the household.

The stairs led down to an elegant hallway with three doors off it. Luisa knocked briefly on one of them and stood back, indicating that Shelley was to go in.

At first glance the room was faintly intimidating, full of heavy, dark furniture and lacking in light, but as her eyes accustomed themselves to the dimness Shelley recognised a richness to the furnishings that muted its heavy authority. A

French window gave on to a small and obviously private courtyard—the sacred preserve of the males of the family, she thought sardonically as she turned to face the other occupants of the room.

There were only two of them: Jaime, and another man who she guessed must be the *advogado*.

She was not really surprised at the absence of her stepmother and sister, but she wondered a little cynically how her father would feel if he knew how completely her new family had thrown her to the wolves, or rather to the panther, for it was that beast of prey who most reminded her of her arrogant and dangerous stepbrother.

'Ah, Shelley, let me introduce you to Senhor Armandes. I shall leave it to him to explain to you the intricacies of your father's will, where it touches upon your inheritance.' He turned and said something in Portuguese to the lawyer, who looked grave and bowed over Shelley's hand.

Resentment shook her. It was all right for her arrogant stepbrother to misjudge her if he wished, for she did not intend to allow the lawyer to labour under the same misapprehension.

The moment the door closed behind her stepbrother, she launched into impetuous speech.

'Please, let us both sit down, so that we will be more comfortable,' suggested Senhor Armandes, gently interrupting her before she had said more than half a dozen words.

Unwillingly subsiding into a chair, she waited

for him to sit down, and then, leaning across the desk, declared in impassioned tones, 'Before you say anything to me about my father's will, I want to make it plain to you that no matter what he has left me, I intend to renounce all claim to it. As far as I am concerned it is enough that he held a place for me in his memories and in his heart. I don't want or need any tangible evidence that he cared for me.' All the anguish she had suffered since her arrival at the *quinta* rose up and overwhelmed her, obliterating her normal control. Emotion suspended her voice, and she had to pause to blink away tears and get herself under control.

She continued grimly, 'I realise that. . .that certain people believe, quite erroneously, that I deliberately withheld myself from my father. That isn't true.'

Quietly and logically she went through the tragic circumstances surrounding her separation from her father, and her own upbringing in the belief that he was dead. Once or twice she sensed that the lawyer was going to interrupt her, and saw quite unmistakably the shock and compassion in his face.

'Please, don't feel sorry for me,' she said huskily. 'As far as I'm concerned it's enough to know that my father cared. That's the only thing any child has the right to expect from its parents. Nothing else matters.' She bit her lip and added softly, 'I can't tell you how much I wish I'd learned the truth before he died, but the couple he met here on holiday who told him about me had actually moved away from the town where I lived with my grandmother. They didn't realise that she had died and that I was in foster-care, and of course my father couldn't know that my grandmother registered my surname as her own. It was quite by chance that I spotted the advertisement.'

'It is a tragedy,' the lawyer said heavily, shaking his head. 'Your father. . .' He shook his head again, and smiled at her. 'I can only say that had he known you, I am sure your father would only have loved you more—were that possible. I think it is true to say that he was, in his last years, haunted by his need to find you, but obviously God willed it otherwise.'

Bleakly Shelley wished she could share the lawyer's simple faith. It would make her own anguish somewhat easier to bear.

Glancing at her watch, she said quietly, 'I'm afraid I have taken up an awful lot of your time. I must. . .'

She made to rise, but the lawyer reached out and urged her back into her chair.

'Please sit down and listen to me. I understand and sympathise with everything that you have told me, but you know, you mustn't throw away something of considerable value through emotionalism.' The look he gave her was both direct and compelling. 'You understand that this family have been clients of mine for many years. I, like them, have witnessed your father's struggles to find you. They say that to know all is to understand all, so please be patient with me and allow me to explain to you a little of the family's history.'

Since there was nothing else she could do, other than to walk rudely out of the room, Shelley settled back in her chair with a faint sigh.

She wanted to tell the lawyer that she didn't entirely blame Jaime for the conclusions he had leapt to. What she was running away from wasn't his contempt and dislike, but her own reaction to it. She had never ever experienced such a strong reaction to any man, never mind one as hostile as Jaime, and that disturbed her. Every ounce of feminine instinct she possessed urged her to leave, now, while she still could.

Instead, she had to sit and listen while the lawyer embarked on what threatened to be a very long story.

'You must understand that when the Condessa first met your father she was a lady suffering under a tremendous burden. Her late husband, the father of Jaime and Carlota, had been killed while playing polo. Their marriage had been the traditional one arranged by their families. When she married Carlos he was a comparatively wealthy young man, but on the death of his grandfather shortly after their marriage, he started to speculate unwisely, and by the time Carlota was born he was on the verge of bankruptcy. Carlos was a man born out of his time, much addicted to the expensive sporting hobbies of the wealthy,'

The lawyer's mouth pursed slightly, as though he were remembering old arguments. 'I tried to warn him, but he would not listen to me. Of course he had told his wife nothing of his financial affairs, so when he died and the truth was revealed, the Condessa had no idea where to turn. It was decided that she should sell her house in Lisbon and this *quinta*, and that she and the children should live in a small villa the family owned not far from here on the coast. The house in Lisbon was sold almost straightaway, but this *quinta* with its neglected vines. . .that was a different matter. The late Conde was not a man who was at all interested in the husbandry of his land.'

Was there a shade of disapproval in the lawyer's voice? Shelley suspected so.

'So it came about that the Condessa and her children went to live in the villa on the coast, and it was there that she met your father. You will know, of course, that he was a painter. It was just about this time that he had started to make a name for himself, and in fact it was I who introduced them. Your father was also a client of mine, and one who I must say showed a shrewd judge of a good investment. There are, of course, those who would say he was lucky, but there is more than luck involved in the making of a fortune from what is commonly called speculation.

'At the time when I introduced him to the Condessa, your father was already a comparatively wealthy man, but it was still his painting that was his first love. He asked the Condessa's permission to paint the villa, and I believe it was from that point that the romance developed.

'It was your father who advised the Condessa against selling the *quinta*, and who nurtured Jaime's interest in the land and the vines. You will have gathered by now that Jaime was very devoted to your father. It was your father's money and his investment in the land that enabled the *quinta* to become profitable again. On their marriage he also bought from the Condessa the villa, which has remained in his name ever since.

'It is this villa that he has left you in his will, plus a small share in the profits of the *quinta*. You must not feel in accepting this bequest that you are in any way depriving the Condessa or her family in any financial sense. Your father made ample provision for the Condessa and her children in his will. . .'

'And yet still my stepbrother resents the fact that I was left something.'

Shelley said it under her breath, but the lawyer heard her, his expression faintly wary as he interrupted quietly, 'I think you will find that the Conde's resentment springs not from the fact that your father chose to leave you something, but from his own ignorance of the true facts. He sincerely believes that you chose to ignore your father's existence, as indeed did we all. None of us had any idea that you were as ignorant of his existence as he was of yours. We have all misjudged you, Miss Howard, but through ignorance rather than malice. Once the Conde knows the true situation. . .'

'No. . .' Seeing the surprise on the lawyer's face, Shelley softened her sharp denial with a brief smile.

'I don't want to discuss any of this with the. . . with my stepbrother yet. I would like some time to come to terms with what you have just told me, but I still feel that the villa is rightfully the property of the Condessa and. . .'

'No. It is rightfully yours,' intervened the lawyer firmly. 'I admire the independence of spirit that leads you to reject such a gift, but think, if you will, of the future, Miss Howard. One day you will marry and have children. In refusing the gift that your father leaves you, you are refusing it on their behalf as well. You cannot know what life has in store for you. When the Condessa married the Conde, no one could have known what was in store for her. She was marrying an extremely wealthy young man, and yet. . .'

'It is different nowadays,' Shelley told him stubbornly. 'Women are not dependent on their husbands any more. I do not want the villa, senhor,' she told the lawyer, unable to explain to him that she still felt as though the villa rightfully belonged to the Condessa and her family. She was glad that her father had remembered her, that he had loved her, and she genuinely wanted nothing else.

Illogically, even now, understanding the reasons why, it still hurt that she had been

rejected by her father's family. It was pride that
had kept her from telling them the truth; she
acknowledged that just as she acknowledged that
it was a measure of how deeply she had been
hurt that she was unable to forgive Jaime now.
Instead of rejoicing in the fact that he had loved
her father, she felt deeply resentful of it; resentful
of the fact that her father had been there for him,
while she. . .

'You will know that the Condessa is English,'
the lawyer continued. 'On her father's side at
least, but her mother was Portuguese, and came
home to her parents when her husband was killed
in the early stages of our last world war. Jaime
is, I think, much more his mother's son than
his father's. He and Carlos never got on. Carlos
resented him, I think, and his childhood was not
a happy time for him. You have much in
common, you and he, even if neither of you
knows it yet.'

He was interrupted by a maid carrying a tray
of coffee. There were three cups on it, but when
Jaime came in on the heels of the maid, Shelley
stood up and excused herself. She saw Jaime
frown as she walked to the door, but he made no
move to check her.

She had spoken to the lawyer and there was
nothing to keep her here now. Her cases were in
her room, but it was an easy task to carry them
down to her car, which she found by asking the
old man who tended the gardens what had
happened to it.

It had apparently been parked in the *quinta's* stable-cum-garage block. At another time she would have lingered to admire and stroke the silky coats of the horses she glimpsed as she walked past their boxes, but she was too intent on what she intended to do.

Two days ago it would have been impossible for her to imagine leaving anywhere without saying goodbye to her host and hostess, but her stepbrother and his family would feel no regret at her going. It was shaming to feel such an intense wave of desolation, something she should have been far too adult to experience.

Her car started first time. The petrol tank was a quarter full, plenty to get her to the nearest garage. As she drove away from the *quinta* she resisted the impulse to look back, and yet thirty kilometres on, when she came to the place where the road forked, she found herself taking the fork that led down to the coast.

She had given in to the craziest impulse, and yet she knew she couldn't leave the Algarve without at least seeing the villa her father had left her.

Luckily the lawyer had mentioned the village in which it was situated, and she had remembered the name. That quick glance at the map in the garage, supposedly to check her bearings, had shown her that she could easily reach the village by late afternoon; there were several large hotels dotted along this part of the Algarve coastline, or so she remembered from her guide book, and surely she could find a bed for the night in one of them before continuing her journey home?

A tiny voice warned her that it was folly to go to the villa, but she couldn't resist the impulse to see it. Perhaps there she would find something of her father, some sense of him that she could cling to in the years ahead.

CHAPTER THREE

THE village lay just below the thick belt of pine forest that clad the lower slopes of the hills, and as the road dipped, Shelley saw the sea, impossibly blue for the Atlantic, reflecting the colour of the cloudless sky.

After the welcome shade of the forest, the white glare of the sun bouncing back off the houses in the village made her wince. In the small square, groups of people sat outside the one pavement café.

One or two people eyed her curiously as she climbed out of her car, but in the main she was courteously ignored. The Portuguese as a nation were much more withdrawn and aloof than their other Latin cousins.

She sat down at one of the empty tables and a waiter came to take her order. Despite the dust thrown up by the traffic that went through the square the tables and chairs were immaculately clean. Shelley ordered a lemonade and tentatively asked the waiter if he knew the way to the Villa Hilvares, as the lawyer had told her her father's property was called. To her relief the waiter obviously understood and spoke English, and quickly gave her the directions she needed. It seemed that the villa was a little way out of the village, overlooking the sea.

There had been more than a slight flicker of curiosity in the waiter's eyes when she had mentioned the villa's name. Since it took its name from her stepbrother's family and had once belonged to them, Shelley guessed that they were probably quite well known in the area as local landowners.

Although she had accused Jaime of not wanting any of the family property to pass out of his hands. Shelley knew really that she had probably done him an injustice. He was far too proud a man to be betrayed by such a vulgar vice as greed. Not that it mattered. She had already instructed the lawyer to draw up the papers which would enable her to return the villa, and the income that would come to her from the rest of her father's bequest, to Jaime and his family, and she had asked him to forward them to her solicitors in London. She would be back there sooner than she had anticipated. She had come to Portugal with such high hopes—ridiculously emotional hopes, she derided herself now. Anyone with an ounce of common sense would have realised that she wouldn't be welcome. But her stepfamily hadn't known the truth. . .

Moving restlessly in her seat, she tried to banish Jaime and his family from her mind. Someone on the next table ordered a sandwich, and Shelley suddenly realised how long it was since she had eaten. it took her ten minutes to catch the waiter's eye, but when he eventually returned with her order, she found the coffee he had brought her tasted hot and invigorating and the ham roll was deliciously fresh.

It was six o'clock when she returned to her car. The directions the waiter had given her were easy to follow, and she found the villa at the end of a narrow, untarmacked road.

Like the *quinta*, it was built primarily in the Moorish style, its wooden shutters closed and a large arched wooden doorway blocking her entrance. She should, of course, have realised that the place would be locked up. With a let-down feeling, Shelley stared at the white walls and shuttered windows, filled with a sense of depressed frustration. She would find nothing of her father here outside this shuttered, empty house.

This part of the Algarve was renowned for its sandy beaches, and less than a couple of miles further down the beach Shelley saw that someone was constructing a large hotel. It was a strange sensation to realise that this land she was standing on actually belonged to her. In Portugal the beaches were all the property of the nation, but the villa and several acres of land that went with it were apparently hers.

It was no good. She felt no sense of ownership, of belonging. If she could have gone inside the villa. . .or even perhaps seen some of her father's work. But she had too much pride to go back to the *quinta* and ask.

The sun was dipping into the sea, sinking slowly. Soon it would be dark. She ought to head back to her car and drive down the coast, otherwise she would never find a hotel where she could spend the night, but something father had lived here in this land, in this very building, but she couldn't picture him here. She didn't even know what he looked like, she reflected bitterly. Her grandmother had destroyed the wedding photographs after her mother had died.

Coming here had been a stupid impulse, a waste of time. She turned round abruptly, tensing in shock as she saw the man watching her.

'Jaime!'

She wasn't aware of saying his name, only of the intense panic locking her muscles. A confrontation here with this man was the last thing she wanted.

'I hoped I might find you here.'

Something had changed. He no longer looked quite as austere, and his eyes when they met hers held both regret and remorse.

He stood within an arm's length of her, but made no attempt to touch her.

'What can I say?' He spread his hands in a gesture that was totally continental.

'Why did you not tell us, *querida*?' His voice sounded rough and tired. 'Had we known. . .'

'You would still have resented me,' interrupted Shelley curtly. 'You wanted to believe the worst of me, and now that you've discovered that you were wrong, you've followed me here to apologise. But it's not my feelings that concern you, but your own, your own pride. You don't give a damn about me, or my pain; all you're concerned with is your own precious pride.'

'You are wrong. I *am* concerned about you; but I am not the only one to be guilty of the sin of pride. I believe it is *your* pride that leads you to punish us by leaving us with our burden of guilt by not allowing us the opportunity to make amends. Your father was one of the best men I have ever known, and I have always considered myself more than fortunate to have him as my mentor in the place of a father with whom I never got on. Since you share with me the sin of pride, I am sure you must know what it does to me to know that my gain, my good fortune, was your loss, your unhappiness.'

Ridiculously, his words softened her resentment and made her eyes prickle with tears. She turned away from him, glad of the concealing blanket of dusk.

'I grew up believing him dead. I only wish. . .' She broke off and stared blindly at the dim outline of the villa. 'I thought I might find something of him here. . .I don't even know what he looked like. . .' Her control threatened to desert her completely, and she knew she couldn't stay here any longer. The dusk which earlier she had welcomed now seemed to promote a dangerously weakening intimacy.

'I must go. . .I have already told the lawyer to

draw up papers returning the villa to your family.
I don't want it. . . I. . .'

She had her back to him and prayed that she
could get to her car without him seeing that she
was in tears. It was years since she had cried.
She never cried, and yet here she was. . .

She tensed as she felt his touch on her arm
and pulled violently away from him, but inexplic-
ably, as she moved away, his body blocked her
path, his hands cupping her face and tilting it so
that he could look into her tear-drenched eyes.

'Ah, *querida*, do not hide your tears from me.
Do you not think that I have wept for him too?'

Incredibly, she was held fast in his arms, being
comforted by the soft murmur of his voice and
the gentle stroking caress of his hands as she
sobbed out her pent-up anguish and pain against
his shoulders. This was what she had always
wanted, she recognised numbly—this safety. . .
this caring, this reassurance of strong arms
around her.

'Come, let us put aside our differences and
start again, little sister. Come back with me to
the *quinta* now. My mother was most concerned
for you. It is still not done in this part of the
world for our young women to wander alone
at night.'

She wanted to protest, but it was like struggling
against a heavy drug.

'My car,' she reminded him, but Jaime was
already leading her away from the villa.

'José will drive it back for you. Tomorrow we

will come back with the key and I shall show you round the villa. If it is that you genuinely do not wish to keep it, then I shall buy it from you at its market price. No...say nothing now...it is something we will talk about later when we are both more ourselves.'

Keeping his arm round her, he directed her towards his car, which was parked half-way down the rutted road.

His manner towards her now was completely fraternal. His comments about his desire for her made the previous evening night never have been uttered; she had been right to suspect then that he had lied about wanting her. Now that she was over the emotional shock of seeing him, Shelley was beginning to regret giving way in front of him. She tried to wriggle away from his side, but he refused to release her. The way he had held her, comforted her, couldn't have been more perfect if he had spent weeks practising. His concern for her had been everything she could ever have hoped to find in a stepbrother, but only yesterday he had been treating her with the utmost contempt. Why had he come after her? Why was he taking her back to the *quinta*? Why was she letting him?

She thought she had found the answer to the first two questions when he handed her into the car and then said softly,

'My mother would never have forgiven me if I had returned without you. When I discovered that no one had seen you drive through the village, I could only guess that you must have decided to come here. I hope you will give us all the opportunity to make amends for our churlish reception of you, *querida*. My mother in particular feels the burden of her guilt. She loved your father very deeply.'

And it was for his mother's sake that he was taking her back. But why was *she* going back?

To find out as much as she could about the stranger who had been her father of course. What other reason could there be?

On their arrival at the *quinta*, she asked Jaime if she might be excused the ordeal of dinner. The day had left her drained and too emotionally unbalanced to talk rationally to her stepmother.

'I will have Luisa bring a tray up to your room,' Jaime promised her, adding easily, 'and perhaps if you feel up to it, you might join me for breakfast tomorrow morning. I normally eat early, as I like to ride round the estate and check on the vines before I start work in my office. You will find that neither my mother nor Carlota are early risers.'

If Luisa was surprised to see her back, the maid was far too well trained to show it. Instead she gave Shelley a warm smile when she brought up a loaded supper tray, which she put down on the table on her balcony.

The shrimp soup was creamy and rich, and after she had finished it Shelley felt too full to do much more than nibble at the delicious salad which had been provided for her main course.

Her sweet, a sticky confection of pastry, nuts and apricot preserve, she left to one side, instead pouring herself a cup of coffee. Sitting on the balcony, she could hear the crickets again. The evening air was balmy, and carried a faint and elusive scent which she could not recognise. Replete and relaxed, she felt tired enough to sleep, even though it was only just gone ten o'clock.

No one could have been more compassionate or more concerned than Jaime had been this evening. Had she not seen that other arrogant, cynical side of him for herself, had she only known his tenderness and care, she doubted if she could have believed it might exist. But it did exist.

From the courtyard, she could hear the sound of the fountain, and another sound: voices. Curious, she moved towards the edge of her balcony. Below her in the courtyard, Jaime walked with his mother.

'I am so glad that you were able to persuade her to come back, Jaime,' Shelley heard her step-mother saying. 'I feel so guilty. . . When one thinks of what she must have suffered. If Philip had known. . .'

Shelley could hear the tears in the older woman's voice, and a lump formed in her own throat.

'The blame is mine,' she heard Jaime saying. 'I was the one who misjudged her, but do not worry, Mama; we will find a way of making amends.'

'And the villa? Senhor Armandes tells me that she is most adamant that she does not want it.'

The sound of their voices ceased as they moved back inside, and Shelley sighed as she retreated from her window. Why had she allowed Jaime to persuade her to come back to the *quinta* when she had been so determined to leave? Was it purely because of her need to discover more about her father, or was it partially Jaime himself who was the lure?

A tremor of fear shuddered through her. She had made a vow years ago that love as other girls knew it was not going to be for her. Marriage held no attraction for her. She doubted that she could ever trust anyone to that extent. She preferred to be independent both emotionally and financially, and yet here she was trembling like an adolescent at the memory of a man's brief touch.

Jaime was her stepbrother, she reminded herself fiercely as she prepared for bed. That was all. The bond she had felt between them this evening had been an illusion—nothing more. She must not allow herself to be bemused by the emotion she had heard in his voice when he spoke of her father, or by the compassion she had seen in his eyes when he had witnessed her tears.

Her tears. . . She flinched at the memory of her weakness. No one else had ever seen her cry: not her grandmother, not her foster-parents, not her friends. . .no one. It made her feel frighteningly vulnerable that Jaime had seen them. Feeling vulnerable was not a sensation she liked.

Impatient with herself, she searched through her case for a clean nightdress and headed for her bathroom. The sanitaryware was slightly old-fashioned and the bath huge, but it was bliss to soak in deep, piping hot water. For good measure she washed her hair, rubbing it half dry with a thick cotton towel.

Without any make-up her skin looked very pale, almost translucent in fact, when she compared it mentally with Jaime's olive-gold flesh. Unbidden, she had a hauntingly erotic image of the two of them entwined together in a lovers' embrace. Instantly she banished it. What on earth was happening to her? She simply did not react to men like that! She never had. The male body held no fascination or appeal for her; the sexual act was something indulged in by others. Her grandmother's old-fashioned upbringing and her own fastidiousness had seen to that.

A twenty-five-year-old virgin! What an anachronism! She didn't doubt that Jaime would be very sexually experienced.

There she went again! What concern was that of hers? He was her stepbrother; that was all. She frowned suddenly as she sat on the edge of the bath, towelling her hair.

She judged that Jaime would be somewhere in his early thirties. Surely he should be married? In Latin countries both men and women did marry early. And the majority of the men still expected their brides to be chaste, especially in this part of the world where their Moorish blood was still part of their ancestry.

Her hairdryer was still in her case and, wrapping a spare towel around herself sarong-wise, Shelley walked into her bedroom. The towel wasn't very wide, and the sight of herself with her hair tangling wildly down to her shoulders and the long length of her legs exposed by the too-brief towel made her raise her eyebrows slightly in faint distaste. She didn't like presenting any image to the world other than a neatly composed, businesslike one. The reflection she saw now was not a familiar one. At home, after having a bath, she normally wore a full length terry-towelling bathrobe which effectively covered her from throat to toes, and she didn't like the wild disarray of her hair either. Again, at home, she normally called in at her hairdressers every other day to get it washed and blown. Her style was a simple one but she believed in keeping it professionally looked after.

She had had the foresight to bring with her an adaptor plug for her hairdryer, and later she blamed the noise the dryer was making for masking the sound of anyone knocking on her door.

When she first caught sight of the door opening out of the corner of her eye, she thought it was simply Luisa coming to collect her supper tray, and so did not stop what she was doing.

When she realised it was Jaime and not Luisa who had come in, he was already inside the room with the door firmly closed behind him, and it was too late for her to ask him not to come in.

'Mama was concerned about you, so I offered to check that you were all right.'

Because she felt it was faintly demeaning to be kneeling on the floor in front of the mirror while he towered over her, she put down her hairdryer and stood up, forgetting for the moment the brevity of the towel.

The heat of the dryer had flushed her skin a soft pink, and her hair, although nearly dry and smooth, still tended to curl waywardly on to her face. The towel, which had been securely anchored when she kneeled down, had loosened slightly, revealing far more of the upper curves of her breasts than was decent, Shelley realised as she caught a glimpse of herself in the mirror.

Other than removing the towel completely and resecuring it there was little she could do. The way Jaime looked at her made her stiffen defensively, her eyes flashing messages of resentment.

'You will find in this country that it is not permissible for young unmarried women to flaunt themselves so provocatively in front of a man.'

His mouth had compressed into a stern line, and he was looking at her for all the world as though she were some child he had caught out in a misdemeanour. Anger flared through her.

'For your information, I do not consider that I was either flaunting myself or provocative. You seem to forget you came in here uninvited.'

'I knocked.'

'I didn't hear you, and if I had you may be sure I would have asked you not to come in.' She saw the look in his eyes and said furiously, 'Strange though it may sound, I am not in the habit of parading around skimpily dressed in front of strangers.'

'But when you are alone you obviously prefer to be free of the encumbrance of clothes.' He shrugged, and added before she could voice her outrage. 'Why not? I admit I prefer it myself. But such an easy acceptance of one's own nudity speaks of an experience that we do not expect or appreciate in our young unmarried women in this part of the world.'

Their earlier harmony was completely forgotten as Shelley turned on him. 'For your information—not that it's in the least any of your concern—I am not in the habit of wandering around in the nude; far from it. It is simply that I neglected to bring my bathrobe with me. What I certainly did not expect was for my privacy to be invaded, and now if you would kindly leave. . .'

Her flash of temper seemed to amuse rather than annoy him, and instead of leaving as she had suggested, he propped himself up against her bedroom wall, and slid his hands into the pockets of his extremely well-cut cream trousers.

'There is no need for all this heat and vehemence, little sister, but you are wrong, you know. You are my concern—very much so. In Portugal we take our family responsibilities very seriously, and as I am your stepbrother it will be my duty and responsibility to guard and protect you, just as I do Carlota. You may not know it, but most of us in this part of the world have Moorish blood in our veins, and that is a legacy that makes us very careful of our women. For instance, were I to walk into your room and find you like this with some other man, as your brother I should quite naturally be expected to demand that he make reparation for your loss of honour by offering you marriage.'

Shelley sat down on the bed and stared at him. 'But that's ridiculous. . .it's mediaeval!'

'Maybe. In our cities, like Lisbon for instance, I am sure they would agree with you, but this is a very remote country area, and perhaps a little old-fashioned.'

'I've never heard anything so ridiculous in my life,' Shelley responded, goaded by his mocking expression into uttering the words.

'Ridiculous or not, it is the truth, and it is just one of the things I have to talk to you about. You will find that in this part of the world our young men are far more. . .responsive. . .shall we say, than the average Englishman. A Portuguese male would not, I promise you, be slow to take advantage of the opportunities afforded by such an inviting mode of dress.'

The cool warning in his voice, coupled with the way he looked at her, made Shelley lash out rashly. 'Then it is as well for me that you have a good measure of English blood, and are therefore beyond temptation, isn't it?'

She shouldn't have been hurt by the way his mouth compressed or by the cold ice in his eyes, but she was.

'If you are referring to what I said to you last night, then please forget it. I should not have spoken as I did.'

'And you didn't want me at all really, did you? You just wanted to frighten me.'

An expression she couldn't define crossed his face. 'Frighten you?' He frowned and then checked slightly, before saying smoothly. 'You are quite right, *querida*, but I promise you here and now that as your stepbrother, I will give you no reason at all to fear me. Now I must go before my mother comes to see what is delaying me. Half English though she is, she would not approve of me remaining in your room, while you are so. . .tantalisingly dressed. Or rather undressed.'

The way he looked at her made the blood run hot in her veins; her desire was an unfamiliar sensation inside her. Far more familiar was the sudden surge of caution that warned her that she was in danger of revealing far too much to him— too much not just of her body, but also of her soul.

'Now you look at me with all the apprehension I might expect from one of our own timid, convent-raised virgins. You are not in England now and, tempted though I might be, I promise you that I shall remember that even though the tie between us is not one of blood, it does exist. As I said before, even in these modern times, in this part of the world it would still compromise a young woman's virtue for her to be found alone in her room like this with a man to whom she was not married.'

Her expression betrayed her incredulity, but he did not laugh as she had expected him to do.

'I assure you that it is true. It is also true that it was one of your father's dearest wishes that you and I should meet and become. . .friends.'

'Friends?'

There was something in his eyes that made her blood race.

'Here in the Algarve we seal our friendships like this.'

He leaned forward, his mouth just touching hers. A thousand disturbing sensations rioted through her. She lifted her hands to push him away and instead, astonishingly, found her lips parting beneath the insistent heat of his mouth. The sensations he aroused within her were all the more shocking for being so unexpected. Sexual desire was something that had hitherto barely impinged upon her life, and yet here she was trembling with the awful weakness of desire, aching with a need which was both unknown and somehow frighteningly familiar, as though some part of her had always known what lay in wait for her.

Briefly she was aware of Jaime's knowledge of her desire; a heated mutter of something unintelligible against her mouth; the sensation first of his hands moving and then of a cool frisson of air against her skin.

She realised that she was naked in the same moment that his hands slid over her body, shaping it with an unmistakable sensuality. Despite the fact that it was an intimacy she had never known before, she was aware of her body's response.

His mouth moved demandingly on hers, his hands cupping and caressing the contours of her breasts.

'Shelley.'

She opened her eyes and found that he was looking into them. He was breathing quickly as though he had just been running, the sexual glitter darkening his eyes edged with caution and regret.

'No. . .I must not,' he murmured regretfully, picking up the discarded towel and wrapping it carefully round her. For a second his glance shifted to her mouth, and his hands tensed on her body. Scarcely daring to breath, Shelley waited. With a faint sigh he moved away from her.

'Sleep well, *querida*,' he murmured softly. 'And don't forget, you and I have a date tomorrow morning for breakfast.'

She waited until she was sure the door had closed behind him before moving. In ten short minutes her whole world had been turned upside down. Where was the calm control she had prided herself on now? With one kiss, Jaime had shattered the defences she had built around herself; with one touch he had shown her that while she might be immune to other men, where he was concerned. . . With a small shudder she tugged on her nightdress and finished drying her hair. Tomorrow would be time enough to worry about the implications of her feelings. To wonder why he had kissed her. Tonight she needed to sleep, to recover from the emotional rigours of the day.

CHAPTER FOUR

SHELLEY woke up early, confused and still held in the grip of her dreams. Fear lingered like an aftertaste of some too rich and tainted food, and it took her several minutes to track the emotion to its source. Overnight her whole world had been turned upside down, and she had been exposed to an emotional vulnerability within her make-up she had never guessed existed. It was impossible that a man like Jaime could want or desire her, and yet when he had looked at her. . . Why was she so frightened? Surely not just because he seemed to desire her?

No, it was her own feelings that made her afraid, her own inner knowledge of just how vulnerable she was to him. All her life she had guarded herself against the pain of emotional ties, always fearing rejection and pain. Her grandmother had instilled in her very young a lack of self-worth that still haunted her, no matter how hard she tried to rationalise her reactions. The only way she could cope with her fears had been to tell herself that she was immune to falling in love, to giving herself emotionally to another human being, and now, almost in the space of a single heartbeat, she had discovered that she was wrong.

To say she had fallen in love with Jaime was to reduce herself and her feelings to some sort of adolescent fantasy; to dismiss them as mere sexual need was impossible. So what did she feel? Need? Pain? That, and so much more.

And Jaime had known it; he had witnessed her shocked recognition of her feelings towards him. She shuddered painfully. How could she have betrayed herself to him so recklessly?

She got up and dressed and then wandered on to her balcony, her heart muscles clamping up as she looked down and saw Jaime striding across the courtyard. He looked up and saw her, and ridiculously, she knew that her skin was flushing.

'Come down and have breakfast with me.'

Shelley wanted to refuse, but to do so would be to betray herself even further.

'If you don't I'll have to come up and fetch you.'

He smiled as though he was merely teasing her, and yet she sensed the purpose behind his mild threat and retreated from the balcony, a fresh wave of heat suffusing her body as his soft laughter followed her.

She knew now that the agonised resentment she had felt at Jaime's cruel misjudgment of her had sprung not from anger but from pain. She had wanted him to like her. . .to approve of her. . . And yet somehow she couldn't entirely believe his volte-face, couldn't accept that a man like Jaime could genuinely find her attractive. . .and certainly not to the impassioned extent his actions suggested.

There was nothing she wanted to do more than to push all her doubts out of sight and forget them, but caution urged her to think carefully, reminding her of the lessons life had so painfully taught her.

Even so, she went downstairs and out into the courtyard, sniffing the fragrant air appreciatively.

'At last!'

Jaime embraced her naturally, laughing when she tensed and looked over her shoulder. She tried to cover her nervousness by asking huskily, 'That scent. . .?'

'It rained last night, the perfume comes from the pine forests beyond the vines. It is a pleasant scent, but it cannot rival the perfume of your skin.'

He bent his head, his mouth caressing the curve of her throat with leisurely skill. Her whole body shook in an explosion of sensation, and she could see the amusement and something else—something far more primitive—in his eyes as he raised his head.

'I could almost believe that no one has done that to you before.' The words were light, but the question behind them was not. She opened her mouth, impelled to make some light, protective reply, but at the last minute her defences failed her, and all she could do was shake her head. Her own naïveté appalled her. She was twenty-five, for heaven's sake!

'Now you have retreated back into your protective shell. I promise you there is no need. I don't want to hurt you, Shelley.'

That wasn't the point. The fact was that he *could*, and she could do nothing about it.

'After breakfast I have to inspect the vines. Come with me. . . And then this afternoon I shall take you to see the villa.'

'But your mother. . .'

'Yes, of course. Very well then, tomorrow you shall come with me and I shall show you the workings of the vineyard. You do, after all, have a financial interest in the *quinta* now.'

'One that I don't want. You know that. And the villa. . .'

'You wish to give the villa back to the estate, I know, but I cannot permit you to do that, and neither would my mother. She and I are joint owners of the *quinta*, since your father left his share in it to her. To let you give the villa back to the estate would be tantamount to robbing you of it. Let me buy it from you, *querida*. I will have it valued and then. . .'

'No,' Shelley answered him decisively, glad to be back on firmer and more familiar ground. 'No, I don't want to take any money for it.'

'Why? Because of what I said to you before I knew the truth?'

That was part of it, but there was more to it than that. 'It belongs to your family,' she answered obliquely, 'and I don't belong here.'

'What makes you say that? Why shouldn't you

belong here? It was your father's home, and now it is yours.'

The words touched a wellspring of emotion inside her, trapping her.

'Ah, here is Luisa with our breakfast.'

The maid was a welcome interruption, giving her the time to get herself under control. It was obvious that Luisa was curious about Shelley's reappearance.

'Luisa must be wondering what on earth is going on,' she commented wryly when the girl was gone.

'I should imagine she is sufficiently familiar with male and female sexuality to hazard a pretty accurate guess.'

Jaime's dry response surprised her. She had been referring to her disappearance, followed so quickly by her return, but it was obvious that Jaime had misunderstood her.

'Does it worry you so much then that she might have guessed that we are attracted to one another?' he teased when she continued to frown.

Hearing it put into words was vaguely shocking.

'We hardly know one another,' she protested, protecting herself instinctively.

Jaime threw back his head and laughed.

'How very British!' His smile deepened, his expression underscored by the faint roughness in his voice as he told her rawly, 'Maybe we don't—yet—but we will.'

After that it was as much as she could do to

go through the motions of eating and drinking.

After he had finished his second cup of coffee Jaime glanced at his watch and announced. 'It is time for me to take you to my mother.' He glanced at her and, correctly reading her mind, said softly, 'There is no need for you to be afraid. Just remember how much she loved your father, and please do not blame her for my failings. She did caution me not to pre-judge you, but I wouldn't listen to her. You see, I loved your father as well, and to some extent I resented that fact that you were his child and I was not; not all my love nor my mother's could ease his pain at losing you. Are you ready?'

He stood up and Shelley nodded mutely, following him back into the house and along an unfamiliar corridor. There was a flight of stairs at the end of it.

'These lead to the apartments my mother shared with your father. At first Carlota and I thought it only added to her melancholy for her to stay in them, but now it seems that she derives some solace and comfort from their familiarity.'

They went up the stairs and he rapped briefly on one of the doors, opening it and gently pushing Shelley into the room ahead of him.

The Condessa was up and dressed and sitting at a small writing desk. In the bright morning sunlight she looked pale and drawn; pain shadowed her eyes, and Shelley could see that what she had taken for pride and indifference was in fact merely an agonising effort at self-control.

Watching Jaime bend to kiss his mother's cheek, Shelley felt an unfamiliar wave of pity for her stepmother.

'I have brought her to you, Mama, and now it is up to you to persuade her to stay. This afternoon I am taking her to the villa, and now I must leave you both to go and inspect the vines.'

'Poor Jaime; he has to work very hard—unlike his father, and yet I think he enjoys it.'

Although she spoke briskly Shelley could see the hesitation in her eyes.

'Jaime has told me the story of how you came to know about your father. We had no idea. He was such a wonderful man.' Her voice wavered and became thready. 'I cannot tell you. . .'

Incredibly, Shelley found that it was she who comforted the Condessa and not the other way round, for who could not pity this woman in her loss?

'It was his dearest wish to be reunited with you. . .'

'Perhaps it was as well he wasn't,' said Shelley wryly, trying to lighten the atmosphere. 'He might have been badly disappointed.'

To her relief the Condessa smiled slightly. 'Ah, now I can see that you are his child. You speak very much as he did. That same dry humour.'

She opened a drawer in her desk and withdrew a heavy photograph album, which she proffered to Shelley, with a hesitant, 'I thought you might. . .'

'Oh, yes!'

With those two words Shelley effectively destroyed the barriers between them. With a voice that gradually grew stronger and firmer, the Condessa took Shelley slowly through the album.

She saw that she took her own bone structure from her father; that he was tall, and that his eyes, as she might have expected, were those of a compassionate man. She saw him standing with the Condessa on their wedding day, one arm round a much younger and stiff-backed Jaime's shoulders. She saw him playing with both Jaime and Carlota, working in the vineyard and at his easel, and through the Condessa she saw not just the photographs but also the living man.

When the last page of the album had been turned, the Condessa closed it and put it on one side before looking uncertainly at Shelley.

'I loved your father very much—all the more, perhaps, because of my unhappiness during my first marriage. I'd like to be given the opportunity to love you as well, Shelley, if you can bring yourself to. . .'

Shaking her head to silence her, Shelley reached out to touch her hand.

'Let's start again, shall we?' she suggested softly.

The Condessa got up and kissed her warmly. 'At the end of the week we go to Lisbon for a month, and of course you must come with us. The family will want to see you. . .' As though she guessed that Shelley was going to refuse, she hurried on, 'Please, it is what your father would

have wished. We are your family now, Shelley.'
'I. . .'

She could get the time off work. She hadn't
had any holidays the previous year, and wasn't
that one of the things that had brought her to
Portugal in the first place? A desire to be part of
her father's second family?

'You must.' The Condessa was suddenly more
assured and in control. 'Jaime will insist. Your
father was very anxious that the two of you
should meet. He had hoped—' she broke off and
sighed. 'Your father was a very romantic man;
it was one of his dreams that you and Jaime might
fall in love as we did.'

It was hard to conceal her shock, but somehow
Shelley managed it. In a bemused state of mind
she allowed herself to be swept along with the
Condessa's plans, and learned that her stepmother
had high hopes of a romance developing between
Carlota and one of her second cousins.

'Not that I believe in arranged marriages for
my children, you understand. . .but Santos is a
charming young man and already very much in
love with Carlota.'

As her father had hoped she might fall in love
with Jaime?

Over lunch Shelley discovered that Carlota, far
from being the shy, withdrawn teenager she had
anticipated, was in reality cheerfully extrovert,
with a heartwarming tendency to speak first and
think afterwards. She also discovered that the
Condessa and her two children shared the sort of

family intimacy she had always envied, with Jaime occasionally interrupting his sister's boisterous chatter to remind her rather drily that they had all agreed they would try to give Shelley a good impression of them, this second time round.

'I never thought you were right about her in the first place,' Carlota told him with considerable relish. 'You see, I knew that anyone who was part of Papa Philip must have something good about them,' she told Shelley steadily.

At the end of the table the Condessa sighed.

'We should have shared your faith, Carlota. I hope that Shelley can forgive us. . .'

'There were extenuating circumstances,' interrupted Shelley firmly. 'And as I said this morning, I think we should have a fresh start. In your position I'm sure that I too would have leapt to similar conclusions.'

'That's very generous of you.' This time is was Jaime who spoke. Shelley couldn't help wondering what he had thought of her father's romantic hopes for them. Latin males had a very strong sense of family loyalty, but surely not strong enough to lead them into marriage?

'Luisa said you spent an awfully long time with Mama this morning,' Carlota commented to Shelley. 'I hope she persuaded you to come to Lisbon with us.' She made a wry face. 'It's so stuffy having to see all the family, but I promise you they'll all dote on you, Shelley. All of them adored Papa Philip.'

'Shelley *is* coming to Lisbon with us,'

confirmed the Condessa, adding briskly, 'and you will not speak of the family like that, please, Carlota. Sometimes I wonder if another two years at school. . .'

'School. . .' Carlotta pulled a face. 'It wouldn't have done any good. You know I'm not academic, Mama.'

'I certainly know that you don't try to be,' agreed her parent drily. 'Now finish your lunch. Jaime is going to take Shelley to the villa this afternoon.' A shadow crossed her face. 'I should come with you, Shelley, but I know you'll understand when I say that I'm not ready to face the memories it holds yet. . .it was there that your father and I first met. . .' The older woman looked tired and drained again.

'I'm glad you have agreed to come to Lisbon with us,' Jaime commented a little later when he met Shelley outside the house. He gave her a brief sideways look and added softly, 'It will give us a chance to get to know one another better, and it will also do my mother good to have you to fuss over and show off. It might help to take her mind off her grief—at least a little. She is not well herself. Her heart is not strong. We feared when your father first died that she herself would simply give up and fade away, but now that you have come. . .'

As he guided her towards the car parked in front of the *quinta*, Shelley wondered why the Condessa had told her about her father's private hopes for her and Jaime. Surely she too was not thinking. . . But no, she was letting her imagination run away with her. Those sort of family-connived-at marriages were out of date these days. And yet there was her inheritance, an inheritance which tied her very securely to her new family. Could that inheritance have been in the nature of a 'dowry', a bribe even to Jaime so that he. . .? But no, she was being ridiculous. He was not the sort of man who would allow his life to be organised for him like that.

'You know, scarcely a day goes by when I do not miss your father. He was a very special man.'

He helped her into a comfortably upholstered Mercedes—a far cry from her own utilitarian vehicle. The inside of the car smelled of leather mixed with the faint tang of a masculine cologne. Shelley found it acutely disturbing, reminding her as it did of the scent of Jaime's skin.

'You obviously thought a lot of him,' she responded tautly, and then tensed as another thought slid as smoothly as cream into her mind. Just how deep was Jaime's love for her father? Deep enough for him to marry a woman he did not really love? This wasn't England. Here a man might marry and yet still maintain a completely separate life, independent from his wife and family. Marriages in this part of the world were not always the union of two people deeply in love. A faint pulse of fear began to travel along her veins. But why was she getting so tense and worked up? Even if Jaime did have some sort of weird idea of proposing marriage to her because he felt it was what her father would have wished, she was perfectly free to refuse him.

But was she strong enough to refuse him? This man had already aroused within her a maelstrom of emotions more intense than anything she had experienced before. In a short space of time she had gone from loathing him to. . .loving him? No! Never! And yet. . . She shivered.

'Cold? It must be the air-conditioning. I'll turn it down, shall I?'

Shelley forced herself to appear relaxed. How had it happened? And why? She had not come to the Algarve looking for romance, far from it, and especially not with this man. If she had been asked she would have said that he simply wasn't her type. Too masculine and assured, too good-looking, too. . .too *everything*. The men she dated were normally far less vigorously drawn, the sort of men one could pass without noticing in the street, while Jaime. . . Jaime would always stand out, would always command female attention.

She didn't want to love him, she realised, subduing a sudden flood of panic. That wasn't what she wanted at all. It was true that she had come to the Algarve subconsciously hoping that she might find the warmth and sharing of a family life that had always eluded her, that she would lose her aloneness, but there was nothing remotely fraternal in the way she felt about Jaime. Nothing at all.

Half against her will, she found her head turning so that she could look at him.

Thick black hair curled into the nape of his neck beneath the collar of his shirt. His throat where it rose from the soft white fabric was tanned and strong, his profile slightly harsh.

'Taking an inventory?'

His voice mocked her, a sensual gleam lightening his eyes as he turned to look at her, laughter curling his mouth as he saw the guilty colour flood her skin.

When he reached out and touched her hot cheek she almost flinched.

'You're very nervous. Is it me, or. . .?'

Shelley shook her head quickly.

'I. . .I just don't like being touched.' Her grandmother had rarely touched her, and had in fact, without saying so in as many words, implied that she disapproved of Shelley's own childish desire to be hugged and kissed, and so as she grew up Shelley had gradually grown more and more withdrawn, until as a teenager she had actively disliked anyone touching her.

Even now, as an adult, she found it very difficult to respond to casual demonstrations of affection from her friends both male and female, but that wasn't the reason she had flinched away from Jaime's lightly caressing fingers.

'Shouldn't you be concentrating on your driving?'

In other circumstances she would have laughed at the primness of her own voice, but now she felt too disturbed by the acuteness of her physical response. Her skin seemed to burn where Jaime had touched her, and she refused to look at him, instead staring out of the window.

They had left the vines behind and were driving through the pine forest now. In places it seemed quite dense, and she shivered a little as the trees blotted out the heat of the sun.

Jaime didn't drive into the village but skirted round it, and when they came in view of the sea, and the hotel complex being built down the coast, Shelley said impulsively, 'It seems such a shame to spoil the countryside with something like that. It seems so peaceful round here.'

'It is a very quiet rural area—or at least it has been, but the hotel will mean new jobs and more money.'

'It still seems to be an eyesore.'

Jaime shrugged as he stopped outside the villa. 'Maybe, but you can't see it from the *quinta*,' he told her obliquely.

The villa was a lot smaller than the *quinta*, and the locked door in the exterior wall led into an enclosed courtyard. Flowers tumbled from terracotta pots to provide bright splashes of colour against the whiteness of the walls. The courtyard was too small for a pool, but there was a table and some chairs in one corner shaded by a small arbour of bougainvillaea.

'Shall we go inside?'

Shelley had almost forgotten that Jaime was there, he had been so quiet. It was almost as though he knew that she had been picturing her father sitting there.

'He used to work upstairs on the balcony,' he told her softly. 'He used to do a lot of seascapes. They sold very well, although he once told me that he painted for enjoyment more than anything else. He believed that he was a better business-man than he was a painter.'

He touched her arm, and Shelley followed him into the house, bumping into something in the darkness. Behind her Jaime reached for a light switch and she blinked in the brightness of the illumination.

Wooden shutters kept out the daylight. The room was simply furnished, but the wooden frame of the sofa had a rich patina and the cotton-covered cushions looked bright and comfortable.

'The villa is only quite small,' Jaime told her. 'Just this sitting-room downstairs, a small dining-room and the kitchen—I'll show you those later. There's something else I want you to see first.'

Curious, Shelley followed him up a narrow flight of stairs. Three doors led off it, but it wasn't those that held her attention; it was the framed portraits that lined almost every inch of wall space in the long narrow hallway.

Disbelievingly she stared at them, turning round and then round again. Her breath seemed to be suspended somewhere deep inside her chest, her heart drumming heavily. She went up to the first portrait and touched it with trembling fingers. Tears flooded her eyes as she tried to read the inscription.

Behind her, she heard Jaime say in a quiet

voice, 'There was another, the first one he did, but I destroyed it. I was jealous, you see, of this unknown girl who occupied so much of Papa Philip's time and attention. I thought he would be angry with me—my mother was—but instead he was just very sad. He painted them because they were all he had of you. One for every year from the year he first found out about you. He painted one every year after that. . .trying to guess how you would have grown. . .changed. . .' He went up to the last painting and took it down, carrying it back to her, holding it so that he could study both her and the portrait.

'It's a remarkable likeness, isn't it?'

Shelley nodded, too moved to speak. Here in this small, enclosed space was the real evidence of her father's love; here in these portraits that he had painted of her. One for each year of her life after he had discovered she was alive.

'The man who told him about you—he must have been a neighbour of yours at one time. He tried to help your father trace you, and when he couldn't he sent your father some photographs of his own children that you were on. Your father said you looked very like your mother. I suppose that's what helped him to guess what you would look like as you grew up.'

Shelley could only nod her head. The likeness that stared back at her from the canvas Jaime was holding was almost unbelievable. It was instantly recognisable as her, even though the hair was not quite right, shorter than her own, and darker, as she believed her mother's had been.

'Do you understand now why I was so resentful of you when you arrived. . .so determined to
believe the worst?' demanded Jaime huskily. 'As
a teenager I was deeply jealous of you, and
although my jealousy faded as I grew to maturity,
some of the resentment still lingered. Can you
forgive me?'

Shelley bent her head. She didn't want him to
see her tears. She felt unbearably moved by what
her father had done. She wanted to be left alone
to study his portrait gallery of love, and yet at
the same time she was frightened. Frightened of
her own emotion, frightened that if Jaime wasn't
here with her, she would break down completely.
How well she could understand his jealousy.

'Shelley?'

She realised she hadn't answered his question
and looked up at him.

'Shelley.'

She knew before he moved that he was going
to take her in his arms, and she moved blindly
towards him. The fierce pressure of his fingers
gripping her arms and the heat of his mouth as
it moved urgently on her own were shockingly
unexpected, and for a moment she tensed. Jaime
raised his head and looked down at her. 'I want
you, Shelley,' he told her thickly. 'I want you.'

Desire seemed to engulf them with devastating
speed. The sensation of the hardness of the stairs
against her back was forgotten in the white-hot
heat of feeling as Jaime's body moved against

her own. His kiss deepened, turning her blood molten, his mouth moving to her cheek and then her throat, his hand easing aside the neck of her blouse so that he could caress her skin.

She shivered beneath his touch, wondering hazily why it was that just the touch of this man's fingertips against her collar-bone could be so devastatingly arousing. Her breasts ached and pulsed, her nipples hard within the silk covering of her bra. When Jaime's hand slid inside her blouse and cupped her fullness she tried to suppress the fierce sound of pleasure rising in her throat.

His fingers were on the buttons of her blouse, tugging impatiently. Eagerly she pressed against him, hazily aware that she should have been shocked by what he was doing, that she should have been stopping him instead of brazenly encouraging him, but the flood of relief that engulfed her when his hands cupped her breasts and not her bra told her how little she wanted to stop him and how much she wanted this deliriously aching pleasure.

'I want you. . .'

The words were thick and indistinct, burning hot against her skin as his mouth travelled down her throat and over the softness of her body.

'I want you here. . .now. . .' His mouth touched her breast, his tongue gently savaging her nipple. Excruciating darts of pleasure pierced her body.

'I want you, too. . .'

Shelley wasn't aware of uttering the shaming

words until Jaime gently released her, carefully fastening her bra and tugging closed her blouse. His face was still slightly flushed but not as flushed as her own, she felt sure. And there had been a distinct gleam of satisfaction in his eyes as he released her. The speed with which he had got himself under control made her feel gauche and very inexperienced.

Why on earth had she admitted her desire to him? She shivered as he stepped away from her, stiffening as he reached back towards her.

'What is it?' He looked down at her, and then, shaking his head slightly, said huskily, 'Am I going too fast with you; is that it? If so you must forgive me, *querida*, but you see, I think I have been a little in love with you ever since I came back from France and saw the portrait your father painted of you the year you were twenty-one.'

'Are you trying to tell me you fell in love with a painting?'

She managed to make her voice sound passably light, trying not to betray her shock. A declaration of love was the last thing she had expected.

'Maybe. Certainly I can assure you that I am not normally so. . .impetuous on such a short acquaintance. You're still frightened of me, aren't you?' he said.

Shelley felt too bemused to lie or to conceal her feelings. 'I don't go in for casual affairs,' she told him truthfully, forcing herself to hold his eyes and not blush. 'We hardly know one another,

Jaime. . .and I do find it slightly alarming to be rushed into. . .'

'Falling in love? Very well, we shall take it more slowly. Get to know one another. . .but you can't deny that the feelings are there, *querida*. For a woman who claims that she does not like to be touched. . .'

Her face clouded immediately and he made a sound that was harshly derisive.

'I think I'd better take you back to the *quinta*, otherwise I might forget that I said we'd take things slowly.'

He watched her face and asked softly, 'What is it? Am I wrong? Don't you feel the same as I do?'

Shelley shook her head. 'No. . .I mean yes. . . it's just that it's all so unexpected. You're not the sort of man who falls in love just like that, and especially not with someone like me. I. . .' How could she voice her doubts, her fears that he was simply pretending to want her?

'You're wrong, I am just *exactly* that sort of man, and besides, I've already told you I fell in love with you when you were twenty-one.'

As though he sensed her bemusement, he took her arm and led her gently back to the top of the stairs. As she turned to go down them he touched her, holding her back.

'Before we go. . .'

She looked up at him questioningly and felt her body burn under the passion in his eyes.

'I wanted you to come here with me and see

these portraits. One day perhaps we will show them to our children.'

He laughed at the quick flush colouring her skin, and bent to whisper in her ear, 'I like it when you blush, Shelley. It shows you are not as cool and indifferent to me as you try to pretent.'

Was that how she seemed? She was anything but cool and indifferent to him. Everything seemed too unreal. Jaime in love with her. . . wanting her. . . A panicky feeling rose up inside her, closing her throat, and she was glad that he had said they would take things slowly. She would need time to adjust herself to the unreality of it all, time to try and believe that Jaime did love her, time to get to know him, not just as a man but as a person.

CHAPTER FIVE

ALTHOUGH nothing was said, Shelley sensed that the Condessa knew about and approved of the new relationship between herself and Jaime, and certainly she now seemed to be taking it for granted that Shelley would be accompanying them to Lisbon.

A telephone call to London had established that there would be no problem in her taking the extra time off work. She was owed back holidays from the previous year, and her boss assured her that there was no need for her to worry about rushing back.

Three days after he had taken her to the villa, Shelley stood on her balcony watching as Jaime strode into the courtyard. He had been working all morning in the caves where the maturing wine was stored, checking that everything was in order to receive the new season's harvest. Every morning they had breakfast together, and by some tacit agreement neither the Condessa nor Carlota appeared until Jaime had gone to work. Now she was slowly learning about the work of the *quinta*, and more importantly, she was also learning about Jaime himself.

She was happier than she had ever been or hoped to be in her life, and yet underneath her happiness ran a deep vein of insecurity, of fear that somehow her happiness was ephemeral and could all too easily be snatched out of her grasp, a sensation that the control of her life had passed out of her own hands—something that made her feel deeply fearful.

Logically she knew that her insecurity sprang from those early years with her grandmother when the latter's bitterness had led her to slowly destroy a child's confidence. Jaime was not her grandmother and neither was his family. He said he was in love with her; he showed his feelings for her every time he looked at her or touched her, and yet. . .

Yet what? she asked herself impatiently as Jaime looked up towards her balcony and saw her.

'I'm going out to inspect the vines. Come with me.'

She knew that he rode out most mornings to inspect the vineyards, but she shook her head.

'I'm not a very good rider. I'd only hold you back.' As always, she was torn between wanting to be with him and her fear that his love for her was something that wasn't quite real, and therefore not to be trusted.

She watched his quick frown, and wanted to call back the words, but it was too late, he was already disappearing inside the house. Telling herself that it was silly to feel disappointed and reminding herself that she would see him at lunchtime anyway, Shelley continued to pack what she thought she would need for the trip to Lisbon.

They were leaving in the morning and Carlota had already spent several hours outlining the pleasures in store for them once they reached the capital. Like any other teenage girl, she was a fanatical devotee of fashion, and complained that the single boutique in the nearest town was hopelessly behind the times. Carlota had also confided to Shelley that she found the pace of life and the inhabitants of the Algarve very old-fashioned. Only last night, while sitting crosslegged on Shelley's bed, inspecting the clothes Shelley was putting in her suitcase, she had confided, 'Round here they still go in for arranged marriages. It's really archaic. A girl only has to be seen out walking with a boy, and unless they're engaged, her reputation is ruined.' She grimaced and pulled a wry face. 'Lisbon is much more up to date. I want to go to college there, but I don't know if Mother will agree. She's rather old-fashioned about girls having careers.'

Sensing that she was being sounded out as a possible ally, Shelley had made a diplomatic response, and decided that the whole matter was something Carlota ought to talk over with Jaime. Privately she sympathised with Carlota's desire for a career and independence, but sensibly recognised that so far she had only heard one side of the story; teenagers were notorious for their ability to be rather blinkered when it came to seeing a parental point of view.

She was thinking about Carlota when her bedroom door opened, but it wasn't her stepsister who came in, it was Jaime.

'What. . .?'

'I've come to take you riding. Don't tell me again that your lack of experience will hold me back.' He came towards her, sliding one lean hand along her throat and into her hair, tipping back her head so that he could look down into startled eyes.

This close, she could feel the heat coming off his body, and a sudden tension in her stomach made her touch her tongue to dry lips, her heart pounding with the surge of sensation his presence always produced.

'Who was it who robbed you of your self-confidence and made you so self-effacing, *querida*? A man?'

She shook her head, too bemused by the sensual stroke of his fingers against her skull for evasion. 'My grandmother. I used to think as a child that she hated me, but I realise now that she was simply taking her hatred of my father out on me.'

'Then realise also that there is nothing more I want more than your presence by my side, that that is far more important to me than anything else.'

Her eyes slid away from his, her senses shaken by the rough emotion in his voice. When he was close to her like this it was impossible to think. He overwhelmed her, his masculinity so alien and outside all her previous experience that it awed her even while she responded to it.

How could this devastatingly sensual man possibly want *her*? She was not experienced... not ravishingly beautiful, not...

'Where is it you go to when you drift away from me like this?'

He grimaced and then the harshness went out of his eyes to be replaced by a certain bleakness.

'Can't you understand what a strain it is for me to have you so close to me, living in my house, eating at my table, and yet not sharing my bed at night?'

The subdued violence in his voice made her shake, her body tensing as his hands gripped her shoulders.

What was the matter with her? She loved him, didn't she? Of course she did; how could she help it? And he loved her. Loved her and wanted her. But why? How could a man like Jaime want a woman like her?

'You're doing it again—trying to escape from me.'

She could feel his leashed frustration in the hard grip of his fingers, and her body was convulsed by a wave of heat.

'Jaime, I—please don't rush me. I need time.' She needed more than that. She needed to come to terms with her own fears and doubts.

'You want time.' He sighed harshly and touched her cheek gently with the tip of one finger, tracing a tormenting line along her jaw to the corner of her mouth. 'How your mouth trembles beneath my touch! Don't you know how it makes me ache to feel your body tremble beneath mine, to hear your soft cries of love and to know that you belong only to me?'

The fierce note of possession in his voice made her throat ache. With the raw sensuality of his words he was conjuring up a picture that made her senses swim. His hand cupped her face, his thumb stroking her bottom lip, probing into the softness of her mouth, pressing against her teeth.

A compulsion she couldn't control made her touch that hard pad of flesh experimentally with her tongue. Jaime wrenched away from her so violently that she couldn't comprehend what she had done; her eyes widened with shock and anguish.

'Don't look at me like that! Have you no idea what you do to me?' The words were grated against her ear, rough with barely controlled emotion. 'I want you. I want you now. I want your mouth and hands against every part of my body. I want your desire and your need. I want your body and your soul, but most of all I want your love, and it's driving me insane not to pick you up and carry you to your bed right now and show you with my body what I can't find the words for with my tongue. Let me tell my mother we want to be married, Shelley.'

'No. . .no. . .not yet!'

She didn't know what made her say the words. There was nothing she wanted more than to be

Jaime's wife, and yet part of her was deeply afraid, intensely distrustful of this gift being offered to her by life. What if she agreed and they were married and then Jaime found out that he had made a mistake, that he didn't love her, that it was simply an infatuation, a dream he had woven round a portrait seen when he was an idealistic young man? Dreams had no substance in reality, and she couldn't bear to commit herself to him and then lose him.

'I need time, Jaime,' she pleaded. 'I'm not like you. . .I don't have your. . .your experience. . .'

'Do you think I don't know that? Is that what worries you?' He was frowning now, watching her with faintly narrowed eyes.

'Partly,' she told him truthfully. 'It puts us on an uneven footing, making it impossible for us to meet as equals.'

He looked at her incredulously.

'I could almost shake you, Shelley. Do you really think it makes any difference? There have been women in my life, I admit that, but none of them have heard me say the words I have said to you. Can't you understand? You're the first woman I've ever wanted as my wife; as my partner both in bed and out of it. Today you've refused to come riding with me because your ability does not equal mine. When the time comes will you refuse to make love with me for the same reason? Are you really so afraid of life. . . of love? Don't you trust me?'

Of course she did, didn't she?

'I can't help it,' she told him huskily, 'I'm not like you, Jaime. I don't have your self-confidence, your ability to believe in yourself.'

'Then believe this,' he told her, coming to her and cupping her face in his hands. 'I have promised you that I won't rush you, and I will stand by that promise, but I'm also going to promise you that we will become man and wife, Shelley, even if I have to drag you to the altar. You possess a remarkable degree of stubbornness, for someone who claims to be so lacking in self-esteem. I think you know you love me, but you refuse to admit it. Well, I *will* hear you say it, even if I have to wait until I hold you in our marriage bed to do so.'

It was in moments like these that she glimpsed the full complexity of his mixed heritage, Shelley recognised, his words raising goosebumps along her skin. Crazily, she half wanted to goad him into. . .into what? Making love to her? The thought shamed her.

'Put on a pair of jeans and come with me now. I promise you we will find you a quiet mount. Inspecting the vines is part of my work, Shelley, part of my life, and I want to share it with you. Come with me.'

How could she refuse?

He was waiting for her in the stable yard talking to the man who held the head of a pretty Arab mare.

'This is Josefina,' Jaime told Shelley, reaching her to draw her close to his side. 'She is very ladylike and gentle; see how she looks at you.'

It was true that the mare did seem to have particularly soft brown eyes, which she had now fixed on Shelley with an expression of melting trust.

Shelley had ridden before but it had been many years ago, on a pony-trekking holiday organised by one of her foster-parents. Jaime helped her into the saddle, while Josefina stood reassuringly steady.

They rode out of the stable yard side by side, and Shelley felt her confidence slowly growing.

There was a very special pleasure in being alone with Jaime like this, in being at his side, listening to his voice as he explained the various stages in growth of the grapes. The crop was not yet ready for harvesting, but she could smell the scent of it in the air. A light breeze freshened the late morning heat, stirring her hair and flattening her tee-shirt against her breasts. Happiness tingled through her and she turned impulsively towards Jaime, reaching out to touch him. Instantly his hand captured her, lifting her fingers to his mouth. His tongue tip stroked erotically over her fingertips, making her shudder on a spasm of unexpected pleasure.

'You see, you feel it too. . .'

Dizzy with reaction, Shelley watched him dismount and quickly tether both set of reins. When he lifted her out of the saddle she felt too weak to move and so slid helplessly into his arms, her back warmed by the satiny coat of the mare, her body wantonly welcoming the hard imprint of Jaime's against it. His mouth moved roughly on hers, but she welcomed its fierce pressure. His hands removed her tee-shirt and bra, freeing her breasts to the heat of the sun. His shirt was open at the throat, and her need to see and touch all of him showed openly in her eyes.

'Take it off for me.'

He moaned the words against her ear, drawing her away from the horses and down on to the soft grass.

This couldn't be her, making love in the open where anyone could see, and not caring in the least, not caring about anything other than this consuming compulsion to go on, to know more of him.

Her fingers trembled as she unfastened his shirt. She felt his tension as she reached the last button, and slowly pushed back the white cotton so that she could gaze in dazed pleasure at his body. His skin was much darker than her own, his waist narrow below the firmness of his rib cage. Silky-fine dark hair shadowed his skin, and she touched it tentatively.

Above her she heard Jaime groan, and then he was taking her hand, spreading her fingers against his skin, bending to ravish her mouth with sweet fierceness in a kiss that went on and on.

Both of them were naked to the waist, her skin pale against his. Shelley caught her breath as she felt the delicious friction of skin against skin, tensing in protest as Jaime lifted himself slightly away from her.

His mouth found her throat, caressing it slowly and lingeringly, his thumb stroking the vein that pulsed out its frantic message of arousal.

He wasn't rushing her at all, his mouth taking a lazy inventory of her collar-bone, his palms flat on the earth either side of her, keeping the weight of his body off her. She should have been pleased that he was going so slowly, but she wasn't. The moist heat of his mouth as it stroked across her collar-bone had become a refined form of torture. The whole of her body ached, gripped by primitive tension.

His tongue touched the hollow at the base of her throat and then moved slowly downwards. Too slowly. Her body arched, her fingers curling desperately into his shoulders.

'What is it? Am I going too fast?'

His voice was slurred and almost unrecognisable, making her shiver as it whispered in her ear. She could almost have screamed with the frustration of having that delicious downward trail of his mouth stopped. His tongue touched her ear and she shuddered, clinging to him as he trailed tiny kisses along her jaw before teasing them against the parted softness of her lips.

She ached for him to kiss her properly. . .to touch her properly. She wanted to feel the hard male weight of him pressing down on her, soothing the ache that pulsed deep within her body.

How could he not *feel* what she wanted? A

deep shudder convulsed her, a need that overrode everything else, possessing her. With a strength she hadn't known she owned, she reached up, curling her fingers into the thick darkness of his hair, dragging his head down against the fullness of her breasts, her body trembling with urgency and need.

'This. . .you want this?'

She shivered as she heard the words whisper tormentingly against her aroused flesh.

'Yes. . .*Yes*!' Her voice was unfamiliar; as unfamiliar to her as the desire driving her, but her shock was lost beneath the pleasure of feeling Jaime's mouth against her breast, not lightly or teasingly, but as she had ached and needed to feel it. His teeth caught the tender tip of her breast and she cried out at the shock of pleasure that jolted through her, stunned to discover that her body delighted in this near-violence, responding to it, inciting it, in a way that made her wonder at the power of her own responses. She wanted this sweet savagery of her body to go on forever. She wanted. . .

She shuddered as Jaime unzipped her jeans and spread his hand possessively over her. For a while it was enough to appease the tormenting ache that gnawed at her, but she wanted more, she wanted. . .

She moaned sharply in pleasure as Jaime seemed to read her mind, his body coming down hard against her, his arousal making her arch yearningly against him. His touch was driving her frantic with the need for fulfilment, her hands moving feverishly over the hot tautness of his back as she tried to express her desire.

Somewhere down in the valley below them a car backfired, breaking the thick silence. Jaime jerked away from her as though he had been shot, staring down at her as he shook his head.

With a gesture that was curiously vulnerable he pushed his finger through his hair, and sat up.

'Dear God, but I would have made love to you right here like an impulsive boy. . .'

His voice grated a little, carrying undertones of self-disgust that made Shelley uncomfortably aware of her bare breasts. She sat up too, reaching clumsily for her clothes, but Jaime stopped her. His hands gripped her waist, and slid slowly up over her ribcage until they cupped her breasts. Slowly he bent his head and gently put his mouth to first one and then the other darkly pink nipple. When her released her Shelley could see that he was shaking, his fingers trembling slightly as he handed her her clothes and helped her to dress.

'Perhaps you were right after all, *querida*,' he muttered thickly as he helped her up on to Josefina's back, 'not to want to come with me today. I think perhaps that until you are ready to commit yourself to me it would be better if we were not to be alone.'

It was her opportunity to tell him how she felt, to admit to him that she loved and wanted him, but something held her back. She felt she was still held fast in the grip of physical enthralment...too bemused by what had happened, by the intensity of her physical desire for him. She wasn't used to experiencing such feelings, and wanted time on her own to examine and consider them. Frighteningly, as Jaime directed her on to the path that led back to the *quinta*, it came to her now she was even more vulnerable...now she had even more to lose.

She loved Jaime, almost too intensely, and he said he loved her; he had shown that he wanted her, so why could she not let herself believe it? Why was she so afraid and full of self-doubt? Because it had all happened so quickly? Most women dreamed of being swept off their feet by love, of being desired by a man like Jaime.

It was just as well that they were going to Lisbon. There she and Jaime would not have as much opportunity to be alone; they could get to know one another slowly.

The morning before they left for Lisbon, Shelley tried to talk to Jaime again about the villa. She was still adamant that she wanted to return it to the family, or more properly to the Condessa, for it had been her home before she sold it to Shelley's father, but as before Jaime brushed the subject aside, frowning slightly as though he was displeased that Shelley had brought it up at all.

'Please do not say anything to my mother about the villa. It would only upset her. After your father's death she was very close to the edge of a complete breakdown, and although she seems to be making a recovery, the slightest thing could be enough to overset her. Talking about the villa will only remind her of what she has lost.'

What he said made sense and yet Shelley had the overwhelming impression that he was keeping something from her, that he was concealing something.

She wanted to question him further, but Carlota came rushing into the room to say that the cases were loaded in the car and that she and her mother were ready.

They arrived in Lisbon very late in the afternoon. Shelley, who was sitting in the front passenger seat of the Mercedes next to Jaime, had been too aware of him beside her during the long drive to pay much attention to the scenery, but now as they drove into the city she looked out of the car window with interest.

It was from this city port on the Tagus that Vasco da Gama had set out on his famed journey round the Cape of Good Hope to India, she mused, studying the impressive buildings and orderly traffic, but all the mediaeval buildings would have been destroyed in the earthquake that had rocked this part of the world in the middle of the eighteenth century.

They drove through the centre of the city and then down a long avenue lined with trees. Jaime turned off this main road and into a quieter one. Imposing baroque buildings indicated that this was one of the more expensive living areas of the city, and Shelley wasn't surprised when Jaime stopped the car outside one of them.

'This house had been in my first husband's family since before they owned the *quinta* and its lands,' the Condessa informed Shelley as Jaime helped her out of the car.

The main door opened as they approached and they were all ushered inside. The hall was large with a high ceiling and very little natural daylight.

'The staff will take our cases to our rooms,' Carlota told Shelley. 'Maria has prepared a meal for us, she knows my mother is always hungry after the long drive.' She turned to her brother and grinned at him.

'No doubt Jaime will be deserting us now. He has an apartment of his own, which he prefers to stay in.'

'Not this time, little sister.'

Carlota looked surprised, and then understanding flashed across her face. 'Ah, of course. I see what it is. You want to stay here so that you can be close to Shelley.'

Shelley felt herself blush at Carlota's outspokenness, but Jaime didn't seem in the least disturbed.

'You're quite right, I do,' he agreed urbanely. 'And one day not too far from now I hope to be even closer.'

There was no mistaking what he meant. Carlota gasped and then turned to Shelley, her eyes shining with pleasure. Looking at the Condessa above her stepsister's head, Shelley saw that she too was smiling at her approvingly.

The panic and fear she had experienced before welled up inside her, and almost imploringly she turned to Jaime and protested, 'You promised you wouldn't rush me!'

Discreetly both the Condessa and Carlota had moved out of earshot.

'I'm only a man, Shelley,' Jaime reminded her wryly. 'Can you honestly blame me for being impatient? I want you,' he told her huskily. 'I want you in my arms. . .in my bed.'

She could feel her skin growing hot, her body burning up with the heat as he bent his head and murmured in her ear exactly what it was he wanted to do with her.

Sexually she might be inexperienced, but that didn't stop her body from being intimately aware of just how much it wanted his caresses. For one wild moment she ached for him to simply pick her up and carry her to his bed to make good all his whispered promises of shared pleasures, but then sanity intervened and she stepped back unsteadily.

Half an hour later, upstairs in the room that had been allocated to her, preparing for dinner, Shelley shivered sensually as she remembered what he had said. If she closed her eyes she could almost imagine how it would feel to have his hands moving over her skin to. . .

Catching herself up sharply, she hurriedly changed and re-did her make-up. Jaime was making no secret of the fact that he wanted her and wanted her badly, and for some reason that worried her. It wasn't his desire she feared, she acknowledged—quite the contrary—no, it was the illogicality of it. She didn't doubt for one moment that Jaime was an extremely hot-blooded and passionate man, but right from that first meeting she had sensed in him a depth of control and purpose that suggested to her that he was also a man who knew how to wait for what he wanted, how to control his desires. She felt that he was rushing her into marriage, panicking her into it, in fact, by overwhelming her with his sexuality. But why? Because he loved her? But how could he? She was so ordinary. Her grandmother had been right when she described her as a plain child, and although she was a reasonably attractive woman, she knew from her own experience that she did not have that aura of feminine sexuality that drove men to desire her.

Why was Jaime so anxious to marry her? Why was she doubting herself like this, and him? What possible motive could he have for wanting her apart from love? She was not wealthy; she had nothing to offer him other than herself, and her father's inheritance—but that was so small and Jaime had so much. What really lay at the root of her fear? Was it just her own insecurity or was it her private dread that Jaime felt he owed it to her father's memory to marry her?

She should have been reassured by his passion, but still her doubts persisted.

She knew that over dinner she was rather withdrawn. She could sense Jaime studying her, watching her, but she felt totally unable to respond to his attempts to draw her into the conversation. Because of the Condessa's English blood, and because her father had been an Englishman, the family used English as their first language, but tonight they might as well have been speaking in Portuguese for all that Shelley actually heard.

It was the Condessa who eventually broke through to her, commenting that she knew that the rest of the family would be very anxious to meet her.

'I myself have several aunts and cousins, who together with their families come to Lisbon at this time of the year as we do. They will all want to see you.'

'Especially now that she is to marry Jaime,' interrupted Carlota with a grin. 'Jaime is considered very much the head of the family,' the younger girl explained to Shelley. 'There has been great deal of rivalry among the aunts to find him a bride. Every summer we are subjected to an endless parade of suitable young ladies.' She rolled her eyes drolly. 'That is one of the reason he normally stays in his own apartment—so that he can avoid their matchmaking.'

'You, little sister, are talking a lot of nonsense,' Jaime cut in smoothly. 'Of course the family will want to meet Shelley, Mama. I suggest that before we return to the *quinta* you hold an evening party for them. If I can persuade her in time, perhaps

Shelley will allow me to announce our betrothal at it. . .'

There he was, rushing her again. She should have been delighted; part of her was, but another part remained aloof and critical. Jaime must know that he was the sort of man whom very few women could resist, so why this rush to formalise their relationship?

'You're rushing me again,' she protested.

He was seated on her right, and he put down his wine glass to take her hand in his, his eyes grave as he murmured, 'I know, and it is very wrong of me, but you make me very impatient to make you my own, *querida*. . . Perhaps if you were to stand still instead of constantly trying to run from me, I might be less inclined to give chase, mmm? Man is, after all, a hunter. . .'

'And woman his prey? I thought most men these days thought of it the other way round. They all seem to want to avoid marriage rather than to rush into it.'

'If it will make you feel happier, I promise you that for the next week I shall not mention marriage, provided you agree to let me take you out and show you Lisbon.'

Of course he knew that she would agree, and seeing the smiles that Carlota and the Condessa exchanged, Shelley could not help but think that by the time they all left Lisbon she would find herself engaged to Jaime whether she agreed to it or not. The thought made her shiver with a mixture of dread and delight.

They were all tired after the long drive, apart from Jaime, who annouced that he had some work to do. but as Shelley was preparing for bed, she heard someone tap on her door.

At first she thought it might be Jaime, and her heart leaped suffocatingly, but when she opened the door, it was the Condessa who was outside.

She came in at Shelley's invitation and sat down in one of the chairs. A faint flush of colour washed her fineboned face, the pleasure very evident in her eyes as she told Shelley how delighted she was at the prospect of having her for a daughter-in-law.

'It is what your father always wanted. His most deeply felt private hopes come true.'

Shelley couldn't repress a brief shiver. 'I hope Jaime doesn't feel he has to marry me because it is what my father wanted.'

The Condessa looked startled and then faintly uncomfortable. 'No. . .no, of course not. Jaime adored your father, of course, but he loves you, my dear,' she assured Shelley. 'Anyone can see that.'

Yes, Jaime had gone out of his way to make his feelings for her plain, giving her the sort of public reassurance that would soothe even the most doubting of egos, and the strength of his desire for her when they were alone together. . . Could a man fake that degree of wanting? A man as intensely sensual as Jaime could perhaps convince himself that he desired a woman he did not love if he had enough reason to do so but surely that would be taking loyalty and love for her father too far? And as for her inheritance... She had learned enough about Jaime's empire now to realise that he was an extremely wealthy man; far too wealthy to covet one small villa and a small part of the profits of the vineyard.

There were no real grounds for her doubts; so why did this feeling of unease persist so strongly?

The Condessa stood up and frowned, and Shelley realised that she was looking faintly ill at ease.

'Shelley, I know things are different in England, so please don't be offended with me, but here in Portugal, an unmarried and even a newly betrothed girl isn't permitted those freedoms that Northern European girls enjoy. My son is a very passionate man.' She looked directly at Shelley and flushed slightly. 'Please try to understand and forgive me when I say that I cannot condone any physical relationship between you until after you are married. Even if there wasn't Carlota, the staff gossip, and Jaime has a good many aunts and cousins who are even more old-fashioned than I am myself. You do understand, don't you?'

The Condessa looked so wretchedly embarrassed that Shelley felt she couldn't take umbrage. But neither did she feel able to point out that her own fear of the commitment of marriage that she would prefer not to be rushed into it, which she felt was what was happening.

'Don't doubt that Jaime cares very deeply for

you, my dear,' the Condessa whispered as she kissed her goodnight. 'I can see it in his eyes every time he looks at you.'

As the door closed behind her Shelley sank down on to her bed. Why had Jaime told his mother and sister that he wanted to marry her without discussing the matter properly with her first? He must have known it would lead to complications she wasn't yet ready for. It was almost as though he was determined to put her in a position where she had to marry him. But that was ridiculous, surely?

She didn't sleep well that night, enduring a nightmare in which she was driving Jaime's car, only the powerful Mercedes was completely out of control, and she was trying to steer it round ever-sharpening bends, knowing all the time that eventually both she and the car would be destroyed and that she was in the grip of a force that left her with no control at all over her own life.

In the morning, when she remembered it, she thought the nightmare had been rather prophetic.

CHAPTER SIX

IN the busy week that followed, Shelley didn't get much opportunity to be alone with Jaime, to talk to him about her fears.

For a start the Condessa was determined to buy her some new clothes, and so she, Carlota and the former spent their mornings visiting the various shops where the Condessa was a customer, returning to the house only for lunch.

Jaime too had various appointments to attend, apparently connected with the business of the *quinta*, from which he often didn't return until the late afternoon. When he did come in he often seemed distant, his mind very obviously on other things.

By the end of the week Shelley had already met a large proportion of the Condessa's family, and although she had been treated politely, she had sensed the curiosity behind the casual questions. It didn't take her long to realise that some members of the Condessa's family had not been too happy about her marriage to an Englishman, and she wondered a little wryly how they would feel about Jaime's marriage to that same Englishman's daughter. For somehow, during the week, she had come to accept their marriage as a fact rather than a fairly remote possibility, even though she still felt the need for more time to accustom herself to the idea.

On the fifth morning after their arrival, Jaime announced that her was taking the day off and that he intended to show Shelley round the city. The Condessa had planned to take her on a visit to one of her oldest aunts that afternoon, but this was now waved aside, and after breakfast, dressed in a cool white cotton skirt and top, Shelley found herself getting into the Mercedes with Jaime, ready for a sight-seeing tour of the city.

In the morning they did the port and its monuments. Jaime was interestingly informative about the history of the city, making her laugh with some of his more pithy comments about the merchant adventurers who had brought so much wealth into the Algarve.

By lunchtime she felt completely relaxed with him, enjoying seeing this side of his personality. He had booked a table for them in a small, quiet restaurant where they were shown to an alcoved table.

Over lunch they talked. Jaime mentioned his father and was quite frank about the fact that they had never got on.

'He was of the old school—he believed that children should be neither seen nor heard. I always seemed to irritate him somehow. He was not a man who believed in sparing the rod.'

He saw her shocked face and grimaced.

'It was not perhaps so bad. I was away at

boarding school most of the time, but I hated to see how he hurt and upset my mother. When he died I was glad. Does that shock you?'

Shelley shook her head. 'No. . .not at all. I felt the same way about my grandmother. I didn't realise then what her death would mean. I was too old to be adopted, so I was moved from one set of foster-parents to another until I was old enough to go to university. It wasn't until I left there that I realised that my grandmother had probably always resented me—that wasn't her fault, nor was it her fault that she couldn't love me—she had loved my mother and she had lost her.'

'But it was her fault that she deliberately deceived your father.'

'Yes, but I can't let that make me bitter. Bitterness can't bring back the past.'

Across the table Jaime covered her hand.

'Your father was a wonderful man. It was he who taught me to take a more distant view of my own father. He helped me to understand that the flaws in my father's personality were his responsibility and not mine. Up until then I'd always felt guilty because I wasn't the son my father wanted. When he was angry with me he used to blame my deficiences on my English blood. He thought I was too soft. That was one of the reasons he sent me to boarding school.'

He saw Shelley shudder and said quietly, 'Yes, I agree. No child of ours will be brought up that way. I want our children with us. You do want children, don't you, Shelley?'

Something quivered inside her, a knowledge
born that she hadn't guessed was there. 'Yes,
very much.' Especially your children, she wanted
to say, but she held the words back.

'If we have a son I should like to name him
for your father.'

Tears stung her eyes. 'I would like that, too.'

'I hope they will like animals. That was the
one interest I shared with my father, but he never
really loved his polo ponies. He used to say that
I was too sentimental. I think when we marry
that my mother and Carlota will come to live
here in Lisbon. Most of her friends and family
are here. While she had your father the *quinta*
was enough for her, but now. . .'

He didn't need to go on. Shelley could guess
how empty the *quinta* must seem to the Condessa
without the man she loved in it.

'You will not have a totally easy life,' Jaime
warned her. 'Luisa and her mother are employed
by my mother, and although I can afford to pay
for help in the running of the *quinta* I am not an
immensely wealthy man. Neither am I a poor
one. The *quinta* makes progress every year, and
there will always be enough money for us to have
a comfortable life.'

'I wouldn't want to be surrounded by servants
and waited on hand and foot,' Shelley assured
him truthfully. 'I want to run my own home.
bring up my own children.'

'And so you shall.' He was still holding her

hand and he raised it to his lips, softly caressing her fingertips, her stomach turned to jelly, her breath leaking painfully away.

'Right now there is nothing I want more than to make love to you' Jaime told her softly. 'Don't make me wait too long, *querida*. I am not a particularly patient man, and my bed feels lonely and cold at night.'

A vivid mental image of the two of them in bed together made her go weak at the knees. What on earth was she hesitating for? She knew she loved him, almost obsessively so; he loved her; he wanted to marry her. Suddenly she ached with her need for him, so much so that she didn't want to wait any longer. She wanted him now. . . today. . .this afternoon.

Without daring to look at him, she said hesitantly, 'We don't have to wait—do we? Couldn't we go to your apartment. . .'

There was a tense silence, and when she looked up at him there was a white line of tension round his mouth.

'No. We could not.'

The harshness of his voice shattered her; the humiliation of his rejection striking right through her barriers, shattering her self-confidence.

'Don't look at me like that.' His voice was softer, but his mouth still looked harsh. 'I cannot take you to my apartment and make love to you as though we were no more than participants in a casual affair. Your father. . .'

Shelley stared at him. 'Why do you want to

marry me, Jaime?' she demanded huskily. 'Because of my father?'

Was this the reason for her unease? Was it because she sensed that Jaime wanted her because she was her father's child?

'That is *not* the reason I want to marry you,' he told her flatly. 'How could you think that? Although I will agree that it is part of the reason why I feel I cannot take you to my bed until we are married. Do you not think I have not thought a thousand times since we met of how it would feel to have your naked body in my arms, of how I would enjoy to give and take pleasure with mine? Do you think I have not felt exactly what you are feeling now, only a thousand times more so?'

She could see that he was angry, and his anger was reassuring.

'Even if you were not your father's child, the very fact that you are living under my mother's roof, that you are a guest with our family. . .I am still Portuguese enough for these things to be important to me, *querida*. In this country a man does not deliberately embark on the seduction of innocence. . .or at least not until after the marriage ceremony. Then I promise you I will make you beg me to make love to you.'

He was making love to her now, Shelley thought dizzily. Just listening to his husky, muttered words was making her shiver with physical pleasure.

'I believe we are having our first quarrel,' he

said wryly, the anger suddenly dying out of his eyes. 'Let me take you out for dinner tonight, and then we will go dancing. At least that way I will get to hold you in my arms. Have you noticed how assiduous my mother has become at seeing that we are not left too much alone?'

Shelley had, and she grinned as she remembered what the Condessa had said to her. Suddenly she felt relaxed enough to talk to him about what was in her mind, although she wasn't prepared for the thunderous look of anger her words provoked.

'But Jaime, I must go back to England some time,' she protested.

'But not until after we are married,' he countered stubbornly. 'Why are you so anxious to go back now if it is not because secretly you wish to escape from me?'

He sounded so jealous that she was hard put not to smile.

'I've already tried to explain,' she said gently. 'Everything's happening too quickly for me. I need time. . .and living so close to one another like this isn't giving me the distance I need to accustom myself to the fact that we are going to get married. It isn't that I don't love you. . .I just need time. I could go home for, say, two months, to settle everything over there, and then come back. . .'

She could tell that Jaime wasn't happy about her suggestion, but she really felt she need a brief period of respite and reality before she could actually commit herself to marriage. The separation she was suggesting was as much for Jaime's sake as her own, although once again she found his vehemence oddly out of character for a man who was in every other way so self-contained and controlled.

'You're obviously determined about this?'

'About going home for a short time? Yes... yes, I am...' She met and held his eyes. 'We don't really know one another yet, Jaime.'

'I know that I love you,' he countered roughly, 'and I thought you loved me.'

'I do.'

His expression softened slightly. 'Very well. Let's discuss it properly tomorrow.'

'But tonight...'

'Not tonight,' he said firmly. 'Tonight is for romance.'

'You won't get me to change my mind, Jaime,' she warned him.

He looked at her and smiled, and later she was to remember that smile and deride herself for her own naïveté.

Although the Condessa had wanted to buy her some new clothes, Shelley had baulked at allowing her to pay for them, and had insisted on buying them out of her own money. Most of the clothes already in her wardrobe were chosen for their suitability for work, and it had been a novel experience to buy silky evening dresses and fashionably flimsy shoes.

She wore one of her new purchases that evening—an azure blue silk that draped cleverly round her body, hinting at its slim shapeliness without being revealing. One padded shoulder had a burst of sequins on it that caught the light as she went downstairs to meet Jaime, the long, tight sleeves hugging her slender arms.

He came out of his study just as she reached the bottom of the stairs, and the sight of him in a crisply formal dark dinner suit and an elegantly starched white shirt made her breath catch in her lungs.

'I like you in that.' Just the way he looked at her was a caress, heating her blood, and making her ache to be in his arms. 'The colour suits you.'

'Your mother chose it.'

How formal they sounded, almost as though he was just as nervous as she was herself.

'The car's outside.'

They were dining at what he had told her was one of Lisbon's foremost nightclubs. Shelley dined out regularly as part and parcel of her work, but this was different; tonight she was with the man she loved.

Jaime took her hand as he led her into the foyer of the nightclub. A dinner-jacketed waiter showed them to their table, which was far enough away from the dance floor and the small band for the music not to be too intrusive. Several couples were already dancing as they were shown to their table. As she watched them, Shelley saw

Jaime say something to the waiter, who quickly disappeared.

The elegance of the other diners confirmed Shelley's initial impression that the nightclub was extremely exclusive. Nearly all the women wore evening dresses and expensive jewellery, and all the men were dinner-suited.

The waiter returned with an ice bucket which he ceremoniously placed beside the table. Two glasses followed.

'I ordered champagne,' Jamie murmured to her. 'I hope you like it?'

The only time she could remember drinking it was at weddings, but the deliciously dry golden liquid that bubbled down her throat was very different from the comparatively tasteless stuff she had drunk before. It seemed to dance along her veins before exploding in her stomach, lifting her into a mood of delicious excitement.

The waiter poured her a second glass while she was studying the menu, but she felt almost too light-headed to concentrate, and instead begged Jaime to order for her.

'The champagne has made me too woolly-headed to know what I want to eat,' she admitted as he raised his eyebrows. 'I'm not normally so feeble.'

'Nor am I the type who considers a woman isn't capable of choosing her own food and wine, but on this occasion. . .'

He described several of the dishes to her, asking her for her preferences, and in the end they both settled for the same seafood cocktail with its special sauce, followed by lobster.

Shelley discovered that both of them shared a preference for fish as opposed to meat, and also that they both preferred to eat sparingly.

Over their champagne they discussed their views of health foods, and the importance of fresh, organically grown vegetables. Shelley was pleased to discover that, like her, Jaime believed a healthy diet was important. He told her about his efforts to grow his grapes as naturally as possible, explaining how the use of various chemicals affected the finished product.

They were so busy talking that Shelley was on her third glass of champagne before she realised she had already consumed two.

The arrival of their seafood cocktail helped to check the fuzzy dizziness induced by the champagne, but she was coming to accept that her life and her future lay with Jaime. Slowly she was coming to believe that he did love her, and that all her fears and anxiety sprang from the past rather than the present.

They were on their main course when they were interrupted by a tall, dark-haired woman who came over to their table and placed her hand caressingly in Jaime's dark-suited arm. Her fingernails were long and painted the same deep red as her dress. Cold brown eyes surveyed Shelley contemptuously, as Jaime performed the introductions, and Shelley learned that the woman was the daughter of a business colleague of Jaime's.

'Oh come on, Jaime. There is much more to our relationship than that,' she protested when he introduced her as such. The brown eyes held Shelley's. 'I'm sure your stepsister isn't naïve enough to believe you live like a monk.'

Shelley tensed as she caught the determination in the other woman's eyes. She *wanted* Shelley to know that there was something more intimate between them than mere friendship. The muscles in her stomach cramped protestingly and although it tasted like cardboard, Shelley forced herself to go on eating her meal with every evidence of enjoyment.

'Shelley and I are going to be married.'

Jaime's quiet words shocked the other woman; Shelley could see that. Her eyes widened and then hardened implacably.

'I see. . .' Her voice trickled down Shelley's spine with the chill of ice cubes.

She turned to Jaime 'Well, darling, I suppose you know what you're doing. By the way, Papa would like you to call and see him about the new development.'

'I'll give him a ring next week.'

As she moved away from them Shelley caught the strong musky scent of the other woman's perfume. It made her stomach churn with nausea. She couldn't look at Jaime, so instead she concentrated on her meal.

'Sofia and I were once lovers, as you've probably guessed.' The cool words were said without emotion. 'Before you ask: no, I didn't love her, and neither did she love me. . .but she is a woman who tends to be possessive over what she thinks of as her property. I'm sorry she upset you.'

'I'm not a fool, Jaime. I realise there will have been other women in your life.'

'Maybe so. . .but knowing about them and being confronted by one are slightly different matters. Had our situations been reversed, I assure you I would have been far from sanguine.'

Shelley looke up at him in surprise. 'You mean you would have been jealous?'

'Is that so surprising? Of course I would, but I promise you you have no reason at all to be jealous of Sofia. We once had a brief affair, instigated by her, and long ago over, but she is the sort of woman who delights in making trouble.'

His words should have reassured her, but the other woman was so beautiful. Why had Jaime fallen in love with her and not Sofia? All her doubts came rushing back, her appetite completely gone. Sofia's untimely appearance had destroyed her earlier euphoria, and Jaime was looking very grim. Shelley looked at him and saw that he was gazing across the room to Sofia's table.

'I didn't realise you were involved in any business outside the *quinta*,' she said huskily, trying to get her mind off Sofia. 'What sort of business is her father engaged in?'

'The construction industry. I sold him some

land that was left to me by one of my father's
aunts. It is much further down the Algarve than
the *quinta*. I believe he intends to build a hotel
complex on it. Now, shall we forget all about
Sofia and her father? Would you like a sweet,
querida, or would you prefer to dance?'

All she really wanted to do was to leave, but
instead she smiled and said that she felt too full
up to eat a sweet.

'Then I shall order coffee for us and then we
shall dance. I hope you realise that the only
reason I brought you here tonight is so that I
can hold you in my arms, without taxing my
self-control beyond its fragile limits,' he teased,
when he had ordered their coffee. 'Because if
not, I shall soon demonstrate to you that it is so.'

Later, held closely against his body as they
moved together on the dance floor, Shelley
reflected that it was no wonder that Sofia had
been so catty with her. It would be very hard to
lose a man like Jaime. With the knowledge she
shivered, causing him to tighten his hold of her
and look down into her eyes.

'Are you cold?'

She shook her head and watched his expression
change, passion replacing concern as he murmured against her skin.

'Ah, perhaps you tremble because like me you
wish we were engaged in a dance of another kind.
Perhaps it is just as well you are my mother's
guest, *querida*, otherwise I might be tempted to

steal you away in the fashion of my Moorish ancestors.'

Something in his voice made her retort waspishly, 'These days women are not helpless victims to men's desire, Jaime. We are able to think and feel for ourselves. Choose our own lovers. . .'

'That is true,' he agreed suavely a hint of a smile curving his mouth as he added, 'but it is also surely true that as yet there is no way a woman can compel a man to make love to her if he does not have that desire.'

But could he *manufacture* that desire? The niggling thought subsided as the beat of the music slowed and their movements slowed with it. Shelley could feel the heart of Jaime's body through their clothing. Surely this could only be real, and her doubts were just the product of her own lack of self-esteem? His hand caressed her waist through the silk of her dress and moved upwards to rest just beneath her breast. Sensation quivered through her as she felt the unmistakable arousal of his body, and with it a primitive stab of feminine victory. He and Sofia might once have been lovers, but now he was hers. Instinctively she pressed closer to him, shutting her doubts out of her mind, aching to be alone with him, to be possessed so completely by him that there wasn't room for any more doubts. And yet hadn't it been only this afternoon that she had told him she intended to go back to England to escape from just exactly this awareness of his sexual mastery over her, the same mastery that she was silently yearning for right now.

She felt his hand move down her back, caressing her spine. Her own hands slid beneath his jacket and she heard him catch his breath.

'Let's get out of here,' he said roughly.

She couldn't have objected even if she had wanted to. They were outside the club almost before she could draw breath. Someone had brought the car round for them, and Jaime bundled her into it with something less than his usual finesse.

Just as he was about to follow her, a small group of people emerged from the club, and Shelley tensed as she recognised Sofia among them.

'Leaving so soon?' The dark eyes swept malevolently over Shelley's pale face as Sofia moved closer to Jaime. 'We're going on to Sancia's. Why don't you come with us?'

'Not tonight, thanks, Sofia.'

Jaime stepped away and Sofia released his arm. Aching with tension Shelley expelled a pent-up breath. Just listening to the other woman talking to Jaime had unleashed an intense wave of jealousy inside her.

They were back at the house far too soon. At the foot of the stairs Shelley paused, confused by her own conflicting emotions. Half of her wanted Jaime to insist that she stayed in Portugal and married him straight away; the other half urged her to act with caution.

Just because they had bumped into one of his ex-woman friends tonight there was no reason for her fears to intensify like this. Jaime hadn't made any attemnpt to conceal the truth from her, and he had certainly not seemed to encourage Sofia, for all the other woman's obvious desire for him. Which of them had instituted the affair? How long had it lasted?

She longed for Jaime to take her in his arms and kiss away all her uncertainties, just as she longed to be able to ask all the questions tormenting her—but she couldn't, and as she hesitated and turned to look at him he swore thickly.

'I'm coming up to your room with you, Shelley.'

'Your mother!'

Her protest was as instinctive and as age-old as time, even as her pulse leapt madly with excitement, but he pushed it aside, muttering rawly, 'It's late. She'll be in bed. Don't push me away tonight, *querida*; dancing with you, holding you. . .'

He looked at her and Shelley knew that she wanted to be in his arms as much as if not more than, he wanted her to be there. It was the wrong way to silence her fears, but she knew of no other.

They walked to her room in mutual silence. Jaime waited until they were safely inside to hold out his arms and say softly, 'Come here.'

The soft command made her jump.

'I shouldn't be doing this,' he groaned as she walked slowly towards him, but nevertheless his arms closed round her, his mouth finding the soft curve of her throat and tasting the sweetness of her skin.

Shelley felt her flesh melt from her bones. This was what she wanted. . .what she had wanted all evening.

'I should stop this now and go straight to my room.' The words were muffled against her skin as his mouth moved over it, his hand pushing aside her hair so that he could explore the tender area behind her ear.

'No. . .'

His mouth left her skin, his hands cupping her face so that he could look into her eyes.

'No what?' he asked softly. 'No, you don't want me to touch you?'

She paused for the space of a heartbeat and then said huskily, 'No, I don't want you to leave me.'

The thud of his heart seemed frantically fast, the pressure of his arms as they closed around her driving the breath out of her lungs.

'Only this afternoon I promised myself I wouldn't do this.' The words were scarcely audible as he muttered them against her skin, his lips feathering light kisses along her jaw, her chin and then the corners of her mouth. She could hear him murmuring soft, indecipherable words between the kisses, but her ears couldn't comprehend what it was he was saying. All she knew was that if he did not kiss her—really kiss her properly within the next few seconds—she was going to die.

In the end she was the one who wound her fingers into his hair, tugging his head down so that she could reach his mouth. It tasted hot, the flavour of his after-dinner brandy lingering on his lips. She touched them with her tongue, savouring the taste, and then touched them again.

'You taste of bran—'

The words were cut off by the heated pressure of his mouth on hers, the frenzied thrust of his tongue making her whimper with delight.

Her hands clung to his shoulders, her nails digging into his skin, her senses reeling. He had never kissed her like this before, with this desperation, this need. Earlier he had seemed so controlled. Until Sofia appeared at their table, in fact. She pushed the thought away, not wanting to heed it. Now he was touching her, kissing her like a man driven beyond self-control.

She felt his hands on her body, moving urgently against her breasts. She could feel their heat through the thin silk, sense his growing passion. Instinctively she arched against him, eagerly accommodating her body to the stroking pressure of his hands. She wanted him to touch her. She ached for it.

His mouth was hot and urgent on hers; his hands slid to her waist as he braced her against him, moving so that he could cradle her between his thighs.

The intimacy of their embrace seared her, her

body moving instinctively against his as she felt his arousal, her fingers tugging impatiently at the buttons of his shirt as she felt her senses whirl frantically out of control. His hands moved over her back. He seemed to be trembling slightly. They moved downwards, cupping her bottom, pressing her against him.

Shelley heard him groan as he tore his mouth from hers and buried it in her neck. Through his shirt she could feel the heat of his body. 'I shouldn't be doing this.'

She heard the raw anger in his voice and felt him straining every muscle to get himself under control, but she didn't want him to be in control. She wanted him like this, aroused and hard against her, touching her with a fierce need that brought to life within her something achingly primitive. She wanted to tear off his clothes and her own. To touch his skin, to feel him move within her.

'Shelley, you've got to help me. Before God, if I don't stop this right now, I'm going to break every vow I've ever made myself. What is it about you that makes me ache for you like this; that makes me ready to kill to have you in my bed? If I made love to you tonight you'll have to marry me. I could quite easily make you pregnant. . .' He looked down into her passion-flooded face and muttered hoarsely, 'Do you have any idea what a temptation that is to me. . .to make sure of you here. . .tonight. . .?'

His words, his almost uncontrolled urgency,

instead of frightening her seemed to only increase her own arousal. Common sense warned her that it was time for him to leave, that what he said was quite true and that if he stayed now—if she made love to him now—she would be committed.

'If I stay with you now, I'll never let you go. . . you know that, don't you?' he muttered when she remained silent. 'Dear God, Shelley, say something,' he pleaded harshly. 'Tell me to stop. Help me!'

She felt him shudder as she reached up and cupped his face in her hands.

'I don't want you to stop,' she told him unsteadily. 'I want you to stay. . .I want you to make love to me, Jaime.'

Once the words were said it was too late to call them back; she could only marvel at her own outspokenness. For a moment neither of them moved, both of them seemingly held in the same gripping spell, and then Jaime stirred, taking both her hands in his and placing one of them against his heart.

It pounded erratically against her skin.

'You've got precisely ten seconds to change your mind,' he told her huskily, but as she watched the downward descent of his mouth towards her own, she knew that her mind was irrevocably made up.

CHAPTER SEVEN

JAIME kissed her slowly, tasting her mouth, and then more urgently as he felt her eager response. Her dress had a zip fastener and she shuddered as she felt him slide it down. The cool air against her skin raised small goosebumps, and as his hands slid over the bare skin of her back Shelley felt her nipples hardening in anticipation of his touch.

He picked her up and carried her over to the bed, kissing her gently on the forehead as he slowly slid away her dress. Her body felt tense with anticipation, her skin aching for his touch.

She lay on her back and watched silently as he shed his clothes, her eyes following the lines of his body. He was leanly made, smoothly muscled, and very, very male. It struck her almost as being ridiculous that he was actually the first totally nude man she had ever seen, and certainly the first one with whom she had shared such an intimate occasion.

He sat down on the edge of the bed and asked her sombrely. 'Are you sure this is what you want?'

'Why? Have you changed your mind? Don't you want me now?'

She saw his body shake with tension-releasing

laughter as he leaned towards her and mocked, 'Does it look like it?'

She was glad that he couldn't see her blush as he took her in his arms.

When he touched her she wasn't capable of thinking of anything but how much she wanted him, and she suspected that he knew it. She had no defences at all against her own physical responsiveness to him and yet she felt, as his hands and mouth caressed her skin, that for all his claims about his inability to control his desire for her, somehow he was keeping a very contained hold over himself. For some reason it was an awareness that disturbed her, but she wasn't given time to dwell on it.

She shivered as she felt Jaime remove her bra, his hands cupping her breasts, enticing her nipples to respond to the erotic stimulation of his touch.

As he bent over her, Jaime's head was in the shadows, but the soft light coming in through the uncurtained windows revealed her body to him in exquisite detail. Shelley felt his shudder as his hands shaped her breasts, her skin tones fragilely pale in comparison to the lean darkness of his hands. As she looked down at her own body, she was feverishly aware of his hands; not only in the way they cupped and moulded her breasts, but also as a separate entity, a part of him. Although his skin felt slightly rough from his work on the vines, his nails were clean and well-shaped. They were good hands; clever, knowing

hands that seemed to sense when to be gentle
and when not. She drew in her breath on a shiver
of pleasure as his thumbs caressed her nipples,
and heard him take a harsh lungful of air.

He moved, his body straddling hers, and the
light barred him with silver stripes. She reached
out impulsively to touch his skin, shocked to find
it so hot beneath her fingertips. His body seemed
to generate a kind of eletricity that kept her
fingers glued to his flesh.

Slowly she traced the shape of his collar-bone,
aware that he was watching her, aware of the
tension growing and tightening around them. His
hands still cupped her breasts but his caressing
movements had stilled as though he waited for
something, for some sign. She touched the hollow
of his throat, and felt its rigid tension as he tried
to swallow.

'Shelley.'

His head blotted out the light, his mouth
moving on hers with blatant hunger, the rhythmically erotic movement of his tongue turning her
hollow with delight.

Her voice silenced by the pressure of his
mouth, she could only arch feverishly against
him. Her breasts were pressed against his chest,
her nails digging into his back. She felt him tense,
his mouth leaving hers as he drew in a tortured
gasp of air, and then his hands were holding her
flat against the mattress while his mouth moved
feverishly against her skin, devouring the soft

silkiness of her throat and then moving downwards.

Her body felt heavy and yet light at the same time, governed by a slow pulsing tide.

'Jaime. . .'

As though she had made some demand of him, he replied thickly, 'Yes! Yes!'

His hands moved back to her breasts, cupping and lifting them to his mouth.

Sensation upon sensation quivered ecstatically through her, her body arching in feverish delight when his mouth closed hotly over her nipple. An abandonment she hadn't known herself capable of experiencing made her cry out sharply, her hands clutching at his shoulders. When he released her nipple Jaime buried his head against her breasts, breathing harshly, his skin damp with sweat.

'Shelley, Shelley. . .' He muttered her name over and over again, his mouth hot where he pressed it against her skin. She reached out to touch him, shivering with pleasure as she felt the heat of his skin beneath her hands.

He groaned, moving urgently against her, his voice raw with need as he protested, 'You're making it very hard for me to remember that this is your first time. I don't want to hurt you.'

'The only way you can hurt me is by not making love to me.' She could hardly believe she was listening to herself, but her old habit of caution was something she seemed to have shed with her clothes. 'I ache, Jaime,' she told him huskily.

'I ache for you here, inside me.' She touched her body lightly and heard him draw a sharp breath, and then his hands were touching her, stroking her skin, moving over her with am impatient urgency that stirred her blood. He moved and for a moment she felt the full weight of him lying against her.

Shelley felt she couldn't get close enough to him, couldn't absorb enough of him into her. She arched frantically against him, sobbing with frustration as she felt him move away.

Dimly she heard him say her name and felt the soothing caress of his hands.

'Slowly. . .slowly. . .'

Shelley didn't want to go slowly, she was frantic for the feel of him against her, within her, and she reached out for him, caressing his body, running her hands down his ribs, feeling the taut contraction of his belly as her fingertips grazed his skin.

'Shelley, Shelley, you're making it so hard for me to remember. . .' His voice was suspended as she touched his thigh and felt the instant tensing of his muscles. Soft hair covered his skin, and she stroked her fingertips through it, lost in a sensual voyage of discovery, forgetting her own needs in the pleasure of feeling how alive and warm he was beneath her touch.

When his hand suddenly clamped over hers, exerting a pressure that almost made her wince she looked up at him.

His eyes were almost black with desire, his

bones showing sharply against his skin.

He was breathing jerkily, spacing out his words as though to speak each one was an effort, his voice strained and unfamiliar.

'If you want to touch me then do it, but for God's sake stop teasing me like that. Just how much control do you think I have?'

She could feel his heart racing, and her own picked up its hurried beat as he covered her hand and moved it against his body, showing her how he wanted her to caress him.

Beneath her touch she felt him shudder and heard him release his breath on a harsh moan, and then he was pushing her away from him, his hands and mouth absorbing the feel and taste of her skin. His hand slid between her legs, making her shiver in shock and excitement.

Tiny sounds of pleasure she wasn't even aware of making interrupted the harsh sound of his breathing. She wanted him so much. She tried to tell him with her body and then with her hands, until at last the words couldn't be silenced any longer, and they burst from her in a tortured plea for fulfilment.

'Jaime, I want you. I want you inside me. Now. . .now!'

His body stilled, his hands framing her hot face, soothing its frantic movements. His mouth touched hers, and a quiver of fire ran through her, arching her up against him. She could feel him hard and aroused against her, but against her wasn't enough.

The shocking intrusion of the Condessa's voice as she called Jamie's name in appalled tones froze Shelley to the bed. It was Jaime who carefully covered her with the sheet, blocking her from his mother's view, before wrapping himself in the quilt and turning to face her.

Of the three of them he seemed the least embarrassed and the most in control. The Condessa looked white, and Shelley knew that her own skin was burning with embarrassed colour.

'I though I heard you cry out, Shelley. I thought something must be wrong. . . I. . .' The Condessa sank down into a chair. 'Jaime, how could you do this? Shelley is living beneath my roof; under my protection. If any of the staff. . .'

'Shelley has been threatening to leave me and go home to England.'

'Leave?' The Condessa was openly appalled. 'But no. . .you can't do that, not now. You'll have to be married just as soon as it can be arranged. Jaime, if your aunt Maria should get to hear about this! You know how much she always disapproved of me.'

Shelley wasn't sure whether to laugh or cry; the situation seemed ridiculously farcical. The days were surely gone when a man had to marry a woman simply because he was discovered in her bedroom, but she had forgotten what Jaime had told her about the Portuguese way of life, and now she found herself listening in shocked disbelief as the Condessa made it plain that she would brook no delay now in their wedding plans.

Without a word being said, Shelley received the impression that somehow Jaime was both amused and pleased by the shocking turn of events, and although he was careful to shield Shelley from any of the blame as he soothed his mother's ruffled feathers, he made no attempt to dissuade her from her flurried plans for an early wedding.

Only when Jamie had assured her that he would spend no more than five minutes alone with her did she consent to leave Shelley's bedroom.

Once the door had closed behind her Shelley faced him with a white face. 'I can't marry you at the end of the week, Jaime; it's impossible. You *know* that I planned to go back to England. . .'

'I'm afraid that's not possible now, *querida*.' He spoke softly, but there was an underlying hint of steely determination in his voice. 'You can see how upset Mama was. She has always stood somewhat in awe of my father's relations, and she is terrified that one of them will find out. If you were to return to England now I could be accused of seducing and then deserting you. In Portugal a man's honour is still very important to him. I know you wanted time, but you must see now that it is something I can no longer give you. Surely tonight has shown you the pleasure there will be in our marriage? How much we need one another?'

Why was she arguing? She knew she loved

him, but then it wasn't her own feelings she doubted, it was his.

'But you *can't* love me,' she protested huskily. 'Jaime. . .'

'No more doubts, *querida*, no more arguments. We will be married, and I shall spend the rest of my life proving to you that you made the right decision.'

Suddenly she didn't want to argue with him any more. What was the point? There was nothing she wanted more than to share her life with him; it was time she put the past behind her, and with it all the insecurities her grandmother had given her.

One final question hovered on her lips.

'Jaime, are you sure you aren't marrying me because it was what my father wanted? Your mother. . .'

'It is true that your father hoped we would meet one another and become friends, but much as I loved and admired him, I could never marry his daughter simply to fulfil his dreams. Surely you know me better than that, Shelley?'

She nodded her head, and allowed him to kiss her before he left her alone, but the problem was that she didn't really know him well—not really. She loved him, she knew that, but. . .

It was idiotic to keep going over and over the same old doubts. She was committed now, and she couldn't back out of her promise to marry Jaime without deeply distressing the Condessa.

Her face burned anew as she remembered the

Condessa's shock when she walked in on them. What made it worse was that the Condessa had already hinted to her that she could not condone such intimacies under her own roof. Even so, her distress and anger had been directed more towards Jaime than Shelley.

As she closed her eyes her last waking thoughts were of Sofia. Jaime was an experienced man. Could he really prefer making love to her when he could have had Sofia? Sofia still wanted him. . .she had made that very plain. There would always be women who wanted him. Did she have the strength to cope with the Sofias of this world? If not she would have to find it. Jaime would not want a jealous shrew of a wife. A wife. . .she was to be Jaime's wife. For once no doubts were strong enough to spoil the flood of happiness warming her blood, and she went to sleep with a soft smile curving her lips.

'Of course, there will be a considerable amount to do. Luckily most of the family have already met you, and already know of Jaime's intentions, so an announcement of the wedding will not come as any great surprise. If anyone questions it, I shall tell them that there has been a long-standing arrangement between you. That you and Jaime met, in England, perhaps. . .'

The brisk way in which the Condessa was making plans for the wedding had rather surprised Shelley.

She had expected there to be a certain degree

of embarrassment in facing her stepmother after what had happened the previous evening, but when she had found the Condessa alone in the breakfast room, her mother-in-law-to-be had come directly to the point and stated that she was not going to mention the incident again, and that she had already spoken most severely to Jaime about it.

'For all that he is an adult male, he is still my son and there are certain standards of behaviour. Even so, I suppose one must make allowances for a man deeply in love—especially one who is just about to lose the woman he loves.'

'He wasn't losing me; I was just going back home for a couple of months. Everything's happened so quickly that I felt we both needed a breathing space.'

'Poof. . .that is your English blood,' the Condessa told her. 'It makes you too cautious. I knew within one day of meeting your father that I would love him. You cannot return to England now. It is out of the question.'

There didn't seem any point in objecting, not now that she had decided to accept the reality of the marriage. She simply wasn't strong-minded enough to stand out against the urgings of her own heart, plus the combined arguments of Jaime and his mother.

With a speed that frankly left Shelley feeling breathless, the arrangements were set in motion. The fact that most of the family was already gathered in Lisbon facilitated these to a great extent. Extra staff were hired to take care of the catering arrangements, and since both she and Jaime were of the same faith, there seemed to be nothing to stop the ceremony going ahead with all despatch.

For two days the only time Shelley saw Jaime was for brief and totally unsatisfactory interludes, between being inspected by even more of his relatives and exhausting shopping trips, during which the Condessa seemed intent on furnishing her with enough clothes to last her for the next ten years. In Portugal it seemed a bride required a good old-fashioned trousseau, of the sort that Shelley was only familiar with through the pages of books.

On the third day, the Condessa announced they were to buy the wedding gown. Shelley's heart quailed a little as she saw the determined look in the Condessa's eyes, but events seemed to have moved so far outside her control that she couldn't summon the strength to protest that she only wanted to wear something simple.

It took them virtually all morning to find a gown that suited the Condessa's very exacting standards, and when Shelley stood before her in it, and caught sight of herself in the full-length salon mirror, even she couldn't help catching her breath.

It was a real transformation dress, a duckling-into-swan gown, with a tiny little waist and a tight-fitting bodice, balanced by crinolined skirts. Nothing could have been more flattering to her pale skin that the delicacy of the silk and lace. Diamanté drops sewn on to the skirt shimmered like tears against the fragile fabric. It was a Cinderella dress, real fairy princess stuff, and ridiculously, after all she had said about wanting something plain, she loved it.

They spent the afternoon in a daze of euphoria buying cobwebby underwear made by the nuns at the local convent, an extravagance that Shelley protested against quite vehemently until she had an illuminating mental vision of Jaime seeing her in the exquisite hand-embroidered garments. She stroked a delicate satin butterfly appliquéd on the back of a pair of French knickers, her objections suddenly silenced.

Shockingly and alarmingly, she couldn't wait for Saturday—the day she would actually become Jaime's wife. She loved him, and suddenly she didn't care what doubts she might have had beforehand; she wasn't going to think about them any more.

She and the Condessa returned to the house in a mood of total harmony, both of them highly delighted with all that they had accomplished.

For the rest of the week she saw even less of Jaime, and on Friday evening, the one evening he was in for dinner, the Condessa had organised a family dinner party. Anticipating half a dozen or so guests, Shelley was stunned to see the formal dining-room bulging with close on fifty people— she had forgotten how extensive Portuguese families were, and she could understand now why the Condessa had insisted on her wearing one of her new outfits.

Out of consideration for the bride, none of the guests lingered much longer than eleven, but just as Shelley thought that at last she might have a quiet hour or so alone with Jaime, the Condessa insisted on whisking her off to bed.

'It will be a long day tomorrow,' she warned her, and Shelley knew she was right. After the church ceremony, there was to be a reception at the house, and then in the afternoon she and Jaime were to drive back to the *quinta* where they were to spend a month's honeymoon. Jaime had asked her if she wanted to go abroad, but Shelley hadn't been keen. She knew that it was coming up to a critical time with the vines, and besides, she wanted to get to know her new husband in his proper surroundings.

She was woken early by an excited maid bringing her breakfast. The Condessa and Carlota descended on her before she had even finished her coffee, Carlota to chat excitedlty about the day, and the Condessa to remind her that the hairdresser was arriving within the hour.

After that the day rushed past in a confused blur, the whirling kaleidoscope that had gathered her in its train only setting her down briefly for a moment in the cool calm of the church, when she and Jaime exchanged their vows. The service was conducted in English, and listening to the timeless beauty of the words made her eyes sting sharply with tears.

It was done. She was Jaime's wife, and he her husband, for better, for worse.

The reception was ebullient and very noisy, the salons full of children and adults. Portuguese weddings were obviously big family affairs, and Shelley was kissed and hugged so many times she felt quite dizzy.

Of course her dress was much admired, and although Jaime had said nothing about it to her, the look in his eyes when he had turned to greet her at the altar had been enough.

She took it off with a certain amount of regret, and was standing in her pretty silk going-away outfit when Jaime walked into her room.

Her room. She shivered slightly. From now on she would be saying, 'their room'.

'Get someone to pack your wedding dress so that we can take it with us,' he told her, kissing her lightly on her mouth. When she frowned he whispered against it, 'I want to take it off you myself. The bridegroom's prerogative.'

Shelley literally felt her stomach drop away with bone-melting excitement and she might have been tempted to beg him to make love to her there and then if Carlota had not burst in excitedly to tell them that everyone was waiting to wave them off.

It was gone three when they finally managed to get away. No one had tied anything to the car or written slogans across it, but nevertheless as she sat beside him in the intimacy of that enclosed space, Shelley was acutely conscious of their newly married state.

Jaime waited until they were free of the Lisbon traffic before kissing her properly. At first when he stopped the car at the side of the road Shelley thought something must be wrong, but when he turned to her and she saw the expression in his eyes, her heart all but turned over inside her.

'It's been one hell of a long week,' Jaime muttered huskily at last when he released her. 'God knows what sort of state I'd have been in if you'd made me wait any longer.'

He'd already given her a wedding present, a beautiful choker of pearls which she was wearing, and she touched them now.

'You like them?' he asked.

'I love them,' she told him, and then holding his eyes bravely, added in a hesitant whisper, 'but not nearly as much as I love you.'

'I'll remember that—you can show me how much later,' promised Jaime softly. 'God, I don't know what I'd have done if you'd gone back to England for two months. Kidnapped you, probably.'

'If you'd taken me to your apartment, your mother would never. . .'

'I wanted you as my wife, Shelley, not as my lover,' he interrupted her harshly. 'If I'd taken you to my apartment, someone would have seen us. Rightly or wrongly, some members of my family hold rather rigid and old-fashioned moral views. I didn't want you subjected to any kind of gossip.'

'You mean if we had been lovers, your family would have disapproved of me?'

Jaime caught the resentment in her voice, and sighed faintly. 'This is Portugal and not England, Shelley. The Moorish blood of our ancestors still runs strongly in our veins. We've got a fair drive in front of us. Why don't you try and have an hour or so's sleep?'

'Some bride,' Shelley teased, 'falling asleep after only four hours of marriage!'

'Oh, you'll be making up for it later,' Jaime promised her, watching the way the colour came and went in her face with eyes that suddenly glittered with fierce male pleasure. 'I like it when you blush like that,' he told her softly. 'I like knowing there's never been anyone else, and tonight I'll show you just how much I like it.'

CHAPTER EIGHT

JAIME woke her up as he pulled up in front of the *quinta*. The staff hurried out to help them from the car, eager to congratulate them.

There was a good deal of laughter and a mild degree of embarrassment for Shelley when she started to head for her old room, and had to be reminded by Jaime that from now on they would be using the master suite. Since this was a set of rooms which had originally been occupied by his mother and father, the Condessa had not shared them with Shelley's father, and although the decor was a trifle old-fashioned and rather sombre, the bedroom with its adjoining sitting-room was generously proportioned with wonderful views over the vineyards and the pine-covered slopes of the hills.

'What are you looking at?' Jaime teased her, coming to stand with Shelley on the balcony, after he had closed the door behind their helpers. 'It's too dark to see anything.'

'I can just make out the the outline of the hills,' Shelley informed him. 'Are we over the main patio or. . .'

'No, this suite of rooms has its own private patio; there's a flight of steps down to it from the sitting-room balcony.' He glanced slightly disparagingly round the room.

'You'll want to redecorate. That will mean going to Lisbon, of course. If we'd had more time. . .'

'We would have had more time if you'd made love to me at your apartment instead. . .'

'What do you want me to do? Admit that I hoped Mama would burst in on us and demand that I make an honest woman of you?'

Shelley tensed slightly. She was beginning to feel nervous and shaky, acutely aware of the fact that they were now married and that she was committed to the most intimate relationship there could be between two people.

'Did you?'

'What do you think?' He was watching her with narrowed eyes, and suddenly all her fears came rushing back, intensified by a strong surge of doubt that he could really love her. After all, what did she really have to offer him?

'If you did, it was a rather drastic way of stopping me from going to England.'

'But effective?' One eyebrow lifted, and Shelley was suddenly terribly confused. What had started out as a joke had suddenly taken on bleak undertones.

'You wouldn't. . .you wouldn't do anything like that,' she protested huskily, not sure really whether she was making a statement or asking a question.

'You'd be surprised what I'd do to get something I wanted—and I wanted you as my wife very badly indeed.'

He frowned as someone knocked on the door, and went to open it. Through the half open door Shelley caught a spate of staccato Portuguese, and when he came back, he was still frowning.

'I'm afraid I have to go out. I shan't be long; not more than an hour. Luisa will bring you some supper.'

'But, Jaime. . .' She looked at him in dismay. This was their wedding day, their wedding *night*, and he was going out!

'I know, but it is something I must do, unfortunately, a business matter that has to be attended to this evening. I shan't be long. You'll barely have time to miss me before I'm back.'

Shelley waited for him to come over and kiss her, but disappointingly, he didn't. He looked at her and smiled, a twisted grimace of his lips. 'I can't,' he told her quietly. 'If I take you in my arms now, I won't be able to let you go.'

She wanted to plead with him not to go, to beg him to forget his appointment, but reality outweighed emotionalism. If it wasn't important he wouldn't be going. She managed a wan smile.

'I'll. . .I'll be waiting for you.'

The smile he gave her made her ache with wanting him, but she made no attempt to stop him when he eventually left their room.

*   *   *

Jaime had been gone for no more than a quarter of an hour when Luisa came up to announce that Shelley had a visitor.

Surprised, Shelley followed her downstairs to the main salon, her breathing catching in her throat when Sofia uncurled herself lazily from a chair and stood smiling at her with thinly disguised hostility and contempt.

'Well, well, the little bride!'

'Jaime isn't here,' Shelley told her flatly, not pretending to misunderstand what the other woman wanted.

'No, I know. He's in a business meeting with my father.' She saw the shock leap to life in Shelley's eyes and laughed mockingly. 'We have a villa not far from here, within easy reach of the new development we're building along the coast. When my father extends it to include the villa's lands, you and I will be quite close neighbours, since I am going to run the complex for my father. Jaime and I will find that very convenient. It's been rather awkward visiting his apartment in Lisbon, but once we're both living down here. . .' She saw Shelley's face and laughed again.

'Oh dear, hasn't he told you yet why he married you? But surely you've guessed?'

Shelley went ice cold all over. It was all her worst nightmares coming true.

'You mean. . .because of my father,' she whispered betrayingly. 'I'll. . .'

'Because of your father's *will*,' Sofia corrected. 'Jaime *had* to marry you to gain possession of the villa and its lands. That land is vital to the development he and my father have planned. Of course, he and I will continue to be lovers.' She looked sideways at Shelley to see how this statement was being received, and something in the former's sick white face obviously pleased her, because she continued in a husky, purring tone, 'Surely you didn't think he actually wanted *you*? A man like Jaime, who could have any woman he desires? My dear, your fabled British common sense must have told you otherwise.'

It had, Shelley thought bitterly, but she had been too head over heels in love to listen to it.

'I'm not sure I understand what you're saying,' she protested stubbornly. She wasn't going to let Sofia completely humiliate her.

'No?' The other woman sat down, crossing silk-clad legs, and studying their elegant length before saying, 'Well then, perhaps I'd better explain.' She glanced at an expensive gold and diamond-decorated watch on her wrist, and added, 'Jaime won't be back for a while. I think I have time to tell you the whole story.' She made a brief *moue*. 'Trust Jaime to leave it to me to tell you! He promised me he would make sure you knew exactly why he was marrying you. Only another woman can understand how a member of her own sex would feel at a time like this. I told him that the sooner you knew the truth, the happier you would be. After all, no woman likes to feel she has virtually thrown herself at a man who doesn't want her, and that's what would have happened to you, if you and Jaime had ever got as far as the marital bed. Oh, I don't doubt he would have taken you.' She shrugged with magnificent self-assurance. 'Without being consummated, the marriage would not be legal after all, and he is a very skilled lover, certainly skilled enough to deceive an ignorant little fool like you. You don't look to me as though you have a great deal of experience, while Jaime. . . Jaime is very good at knowing what a woman wants. . .what she needs. . .'

Sick with mortification, Shelley recognised the satisfied, reminiscent look in Sofia's eyes. 'How sad for you that the only thing Jaime wants from you is the villa.'

'He could have had that without marrying me,' Shelley told her antagonist. 'He knew that, even if you didn't. I wanted to give it back to his mother.' She had hoped to deflate Sofia's hard ego, but her words just bounced off the other woman's exterior, leaving no impression.

'Giving the villa back to the Condessa was not what Jaime wanted you to do. She is adamant about not selling it. The Condessa is as opposed to Jaime's and my father's plans for the land it stands on as your father was—and as stupidly short-sighted.' Her deeply glossed lips curled slightly. 'Both of them are fools. Jaime will make a fortune from this development with my father.'

Why was she sitting here listening to this, why didn't she just get up and walk out right now?

Because her pride wouldn't let her run from her pain, that's why, Shelley acknowledged bitterly.

'My father plans to extend his existing hotel complex to include the villa's lands. He wants to build a modern sports complex to accommodate the hotel guests: private chalets, tennis courts. When he has finished here, this part of the Algarve coast will be a Mecca for those holidaymakers with the money to enjoy it.'

The mental image she was painting shocked and sickened Shelley. She liked the coastline as it was now, unspoilt and homely. Surely Jaime couldn't really want that sort of development right on the doorstep of the *quinta*, but almost as though she read her mind Sofia continued coolly. 'Of course Jaime will sell the *quinta*—that does belong to him. No doubt he'll buy a house in the country somewhere for you and his family, while he and I. . .' She laughed at Shelley's expression. 'You think that either of us would allow this marriage to interfere with our relationship?' She shook her glossy dark head. 'Jaime needs me in his life as much as he needs you.'

'But he hasn't married you,' Shelley pointed out with a coolness she was far from feeling.

Sofia's dark eyebrows rose. 'I don't want marriage from him—or any other man. I prefer my freedom. But that doesn't mean that I no longer want Jaime as my lover—I do. Just as he wants me, no matter what he might have told you. Do you honestly think you can replace me in his bed?'

Shelley knew that her expression had given her away.

'Does Jaime know that you've come here to tell me all this?' she tried to counter.

Sofia didn't even blink. 'Of course,' she told her scornfully. 'Right at this moment he and my father will be celebrating the successful completion of their plans.'

If all Jaime had wanted from her was the villa, why go through this appalling charade? Why not simply. . .

Ask her to give it to him? Shelley's mouth compressed. He would have known that, like his mother, she could never have allowed the villa to be destroyed and the land built upon. And yet he had seemed so genuine and caring when he had talked to her about her father, when he had told her of his love and respect for him.

'If Jaime needs that land so badly, surely he could have convinced the Condessa?' Shelley protested, unwilling to believe that Sofia was telling her the truth. Even though she had always suspected at the back of her mind that Jaime did have some ulterior motive for pretending to care for her, now that her suspicions were being confirmed she found herself fighting hard to reject them—and Sofia's claims.

'The Condessa would never give her agreement.' Sofia's voice was harsh. 'She is obsessed with the idea of preserving the villa because it was once the home of her husband. She will never agree. Jaime expected that your father would will the villa to him, and it was on that basis that he originally entered the contract with my father. See, I have brought it here to show you.'

She opened the bag she was carrying and threw down a heavy bundle of typed papers, thrusting them in front of Shelley's tormented eyes. Of course, it was all in Portuguese, but unmistakable and quite, quite damning, at the bottom of the contract were the typed names of Jaime and Sofia's father—and the document was signed.

'Now do you believe me?'

Triumph glittered in Sofia's dark eyes, and Shelley fought for self-control. She badly wanted to be sick, to run from this nightmare and go on running until she woke up in sanity and reality, but this was reality.

Why the shock? she goaded herself; she had been worried all along that Jaime's feelings weren't genuine. But she had never, never dreamed of anything like this, her tormented heart protested; she had suspected Jaime of allowing himself to believe he loved her because of the strength of his feelings for her father, never even guessing at the truth. She would never have believed him guilty of this degree of duplicity and dishonesty if Sofia hadn't revealed the truth to her.

Sofia was watching her closely. There was an unmistakable degree of tension about her stance that brought home to Shelley just what was happening. Sofia and Jaime were lovers. Oh, it had been clever of Jaime to admit that much to her;

it had thrown her off the scent completely. She had thought their affair was over, something that had not even touched Jaime's heart at all, but now she was learning better.

And Sofia was claiming that the affair was going to continue. No wonder Jaime hadn't been able to tell her where he was going! No wonder he had been so eager to leave her. Sofia was right about one thing. Shelley could never match her sexual skill in bed. Nor would she try to, she decided grimly. Jaime had married her, but marriages could be dissolved, especially when they had never been consummated. She would refuse to sleep with him. He would probably be relieved, if it wasn't for the fact that he would probably have no legal claims on the villa and its lands if the marriage wasn't legal. She couldn't sleep with him now. . .couldn't touch him or allow him to touch her now that she knew the truth. Why on earth hadn't she listened to what her brain had been trying to tell her? It had been right all along. No wonder Jaime hadn't wanted her to go back to England!

Another thought crept into her mind. Would he have *let* her go back? Had he known that his mother was all too likely to interrupt them?

Sofia was picking up her things and heading for the door; as she reached it Shelley said coldly, 'Do you want me to tell Jaime that you've done his dirty work for him?'

The other woman turned in the doorway and smiled mockingly at her. 'That's up to you, my dear.' A calculating, assessing look hardened her eyes, but Shelley didn't notice it; she was too busy trying to suppress her tears. 'Frankly, in your shoes, I wouldn't wait around for him to come back—I'd be on the first plane out of the country. Or don't you have that much pride?'

Oh, she had pride all right. Too much to turn tail and run. No, she would simply tell Jaime that she was not going to live with him as his wife, and as soon as she got the chance she was going to go and see the attorney and see what she could do about setting in motion an annulment of their marriage. One thing she was sure of, and that was that she wasn't going to let Jaime take the villa away from her. Her father hadn't wanted that land built on or sold, and neither did the Condessa, and perhaps that was even why it had been left to her. Well if that was the reason behind her father's bequest she wasn't going to betray the trust he had put in her. Jaime might think he had her where he wanted her, but he was soon going to learn better.

It wasn't much more than half an hour after Sofia's departure that he came back. He was frowning when he walked into the salon, his expression unexpectedly harsh.

'Maria tells me that Sofia called here. What did she want?'

'Why, just to congratulate us on our marriage, of course.' Two could play these lying games. 'I hadn't realised that her father had business interests locally.'

'He owns that hotel complex being built further down the beach. As a matter of fact, he was the person I had to go and see.'

'Oh.' She was a better actress than she had ever dreamed, Shelley thought bitterly; she certainly seemed to be deceiving Jaime. 'Was everything concluded to your satisfaction?'

His eyebrows shot up at her choice of words. 'You could say that.' His voice was clipped, and harsh as he burst out, 'For God's sake, Shelley, we're on our honeymoon; I don't want to discuss my business affairs with you.'

I'll just bet you don't, Shelley thought sourly.

'No.' She got up and gave him a sweetly acid smile, as she walked towards the door. Once there she paused and turned round, her voice innocent of all expression as she asked softly. 'Jaime, would you have let me go back to London—if your mother hadn't interrupted us, I mean?'

'Let you go back?' His voice was rough. 'No way, you know that. . .'

Yes, she knew it, and now she knew why. She turned away so that he wouldn't see the agony in her eyes.

'Why don't you. . .'

She turned back to face him once she had herself under control, praying she wouldn't break down.

'Jaime, I can't sleep with you tonight. . .or at

all at the moment. . .I'm too confused. I. . .I need time. . .'

Time to get their marriage annulled. Time to hide from the humiliation he had caused her. It was obvious from his incredulous expression that he had no idea what Sofia had really said to her. Shelley wasn't surprised. For all Sofia's claims, Jaime wasn't the sort of man who would shrink from doing his own dirty work. No doubt he had planned to keep her in ignorance as long as he could, but Sofia had taken matters into her own hands. The Portuguese woman would be a very jealous lover, Shelley guessed, and would resent any relationship Jaime might have with anyone else, even one such as hers. She sensed that Sofia had wanted her to leave, but she wasn't going to do that until she had made sure exactly what the legal position was with the villa. Did married women retain their own property under Portuguese law? Would the fact that the marriage hadn't been consummated mean that the property remained hers? Knowing what she did now, she wouldn't put it past Jaime to overwhelm her sexually simply so that he could make sure that ownership of the villa did pass to him. That was after all the reason for this whole farce.

Right now, though, Jaime was looking at her as though he couldn't believe his ears.

'What the hell is this?' he demanded roughly, coming towards her, but stopping short of actually touching her. 'Shelley, what's happened to you? When I left here you were looking at me as though you couldn't wait for us to be together, and now you're telling me that. . .that. . .'

'That I won't make love with you,' she supplemented for him. 'I'm sorry, Jaime, but I just can't. I did ask you not to rush me into marriage,' she reminded him.

'Shelley!' He looked both incredulous and pleading. 'Shelley, please. . .I can understand your fears, but I promise you. . .'

'Jaime, it's no good!' She was rapidly approaching a state of hysteria. If this didn't stop soon she'd be blurting out the truth, and that wasn't what she wanted. If she was honest with herself, she didn't trust herself to be able to resist him if he were to turn the full heat of his sexual mastery on her. The galling truth was that despite everything Sofia had told her, part of her still ached for him, still loved him, and that frightened her. She must keep him at a distance. She had to.

As though he too recognised her near hysteria, Jaime stepped back from her and said soothingly, 'All right, tonight I'll sleep in my old room, but we've got to talk about this, Shelley. There's something wrong here somewhere, something more to this than you're telling me. Does it have anything to do with Sofia?' he asked sharply.

Her heart leapt in her chest like a landed salmon. 'You told me your affair with her was over.'

'Yes.' He sounded impatient now. 'So. . .did she say something to upset you? Something that activated that mammoth lack of self-worth of yours, is that it?'

Dear God, he should have been on the stage. He seemed so concerned. . .he knew her so well.

'Did she hurt you in some way, Shelley?'

Here was her chance, her heart pounded suffocatingly as she asked huskily, 'How could she?'

Please God, let him tell her the truth now. If he did. . .but no, he was frowning at her, watching her with narrowed eyes.

'I don't know,' he lied slowly. 'You tell me. . .'

'I don't want to talk about Sofia, or anyone else, Jaime,' she told him miserably, 'I just want to go to bed.'

'Alone,' he agreed acidly. 'Very well, I don't intend to force you to share it with me, Shelley, nor have I got the patience right at this moment in time to coax you to let me make love to you. You're scarcely flattering to me; I hope you realise that. What is it? Just bridal nerves, or have you discovered that you don't love me after all?'

It was her perfect get out, and she seized hold of it gratefully, unaware of the expression in his eyes as she said breathlessly, 'I'm not sure what I feel, Jaime. You rushed me into this marriage before I wanted it, you know that. . .'

'Oh, so it's all my fault, is it? Very well then, sleep on your own if that's what you want. But you can't change the fact that you are my wife, Shelley; nothing can change that. . .'

Oh yes, it could, but only as long as their marriage remained unconsummated, but she wasn't going to remind him of that right now. No, she'd wait until she was sure of her ground legally before she threw that one at him. Luck was on Shelley's side: a freak thunderstorm in the night caused such damage to the vines that Jaime was up and gone long before she surfaced the next morning. He was gone for most of the day, and if any of the staff found it odd that the newly married couple were occupying different rooms, none of them showed it to Shelley.

She had anticipated that Jaime would lose no time in trying to persuade her to sleep with him, but he made no attempt to do so at all, treating her with a cold distance that made her wonder if secretly he was not rather relieved to be spared the boredom of having to make love to an inexperienced and undesirable wife. No doubt he was counting the days until he could safely see Sofia again, she thought bitterly, and when, four days after they had returned from Lisbon, he announced that he had to go back to attend to some urgent business, she thought she knew exactly what that business would be.

'Good,' she responded sweetly when he told her. 'I'd like to come to Lisbon with you; I could spend the day with your mother.' And she might also get an opportunity to go and speak to the lawyer. She was beginning to feel very much on edge. It was a constant strain living like this. And worst of all to bear was the knowledge that she still loved Jaime quite desperately. She wanted him physically as well, and she hated herself for that.

Her instinctive reaction when Sofia had told

her the real reason Jaime had married her had been to leave him immediately, but she had sensed that this was exactly what the other woman had hoped for, and additionally, over and above the agony of her own betrayal, there had been her determination to stop Jaime from selling her father's land.

Her refusal to sleep with him had been born of her own feeling of self-revulsion as much as of her desire to thwart him, and now, after four days of being married and yet not a wife, she was as tense as a too tightly drawn violin string. She wasn't sure what she had expected: pleading, coaxing, a complete refusal on Jaime's part to accept her rejection, perhaps. Certainly she had not anticipated the icy rage she had glimpsed once or twice in his eyes before he concealed it from her. She was the one with the right to be angry, not he. Surely he must have guessed what Sofia had told her, and yet he had made no attempt to talk to her about it. Well, she certainly wasn't going to broach the subject with him. What had she really wanted, she jeered to herself, a passionate denial of everything Sofia had said?

Surely his very lack of the slightest degree of desire for her showed her the truth? Sofia was right. He *was* very skilled at playing the convincing lover. He had certainly convinced her that, sexually at least, he had wanted her. Had it been Sofia he had been imagining he was holding in his arms, and touching every time he... Sweat broke out on her forehead and she felt acutely sick. She couldn't endure any more of this. If she didn't resolve matters soon she was all too likely to break down completely and humiliate herself even further.

On the Thursday after their wedding they left for Lisbon early in the morning. The drive was accomplished in a heavy silence which did nothing to alleviate Shelley's already tense condition.

He dropped her outside the Condessa's Lisbon house, with the curt announcement that he would not come in.

'One look at our faces would be enough to make Mama instantly suspicious. She has enough to bear as it is.'

The look on his face left Shelley in no doubts about whom he blamed for their estrangement. How could he dare to play the injured party so diabolically well, when he must know she knew the truth? As she released her seat belt he leaned across her to release her door catch. Instantly she recoiled, and then quaked in her shoes as she saw the fury tightening his mouth.

'It's all right, I'm not about to rape you here in front of my mother's front door,' he told her savagely. 'Or is that what you wanted, Shelley, to be forced to. . .'

She got out of the car before he could finish speaking, sickened and shocked by the miasma of barely controlled violence inside the car, generated as much by her as it was by him. She almost wished he *had* touched her, then at least she could have had the physical release of hitting him.

The Condessa was expecting her. Jaime had telephoned her the previous evening. She welcomed Shelley with open arms and then drew away, a shocked exclamation leaving her lips as she saw her wan face.

'Shelley, my dear. . .what is it? Have you and Jaime quarrelled?'

So much for concealing the truth from her, Shelley thought tiredly. All at once it was too much for her to bear alone any longer. Tears weren't far away, as she subsided into a chair and gulped painfully, 'Worse than that—I've found out exactly why Jaime married me.'

Bit by bit the Condessa dragged the whole story out of her. When at last Shelley had finished, her stepmother was as pale as she was herself.

'No,' she said at last. 'I knew there was some sort of relationship between Jaime and Sofia, of course. One does not expect a man of his age to live the life of a monk, after all,' she added with motherly dignity, 'but this other. . .this claim of hers that Jaime intends to sell the villa and its land to her father. I knew he wanted it, of course. He approached your father about it some time ago. . .but Jaime knows quite well how both your father and I felt about the unchecked development of the Algarve coast. He knows we would never, ever sell that land to Sofia's father. And neither, I am sure, would Jaime. No, Shelley, my dear,

I'm sure that Sofia has lied to you.'

'But why. . .for what purpose?'

'Perhaps because she is jealous of you,' the Condessa suggested shrewdly. 'She is as very hard young woman, and one I would never have wanted to see married to Jaime, but she was quite relentless in her pursuit of him.'

'According to her she and Jaime are still lovers,' Shelley said in a low voice.

'Did you tell him about what she had said to you, Shelley? Have you discussed it with him?'

Shelley shook her head. 'No, but he must realise that I know. She. . . Sofia called round while he was out—he had to go out on business the evening we arrived back at the *quinta*. Sofia said he had gone to meet her father. . .to tell him that our marriage meant that their plans could go ahead. She told me Jaime had never wanted me. When he came back I couldn't talk to him about it, I was too afraid that he would convince me that she was lying. If he had. . .if. . .if. . . Oh, can't you see, that if I'd let him convince me that night, I'd never have felt I really knew the truth? Now I know it must be true. He hasn't made any attempt to. . .to put our marriage on a normal footing.'

The Condessa looked appalled, whether by Shelley's revelations about her son, or by what Shelley herself had done, Shelley had no way of knowing.

'But you must have given him some reason. . . some explanation for. . .'

PASSIONATE RELATIONSHIP 173

'For not sleeping with him?' Shelley sighed.
'Yes, I told him that I felt that he'd rushed me
into marriage before I was ready. I. . .must go
and see the *advogado*,' she said huskily. 'I need
to know exactly where I stand legally. I've no
idea of the legalities affecting married women's
property in Portugal. . .and then there's the matter of having our marriage annulled. I'm not
going to let him sell my father's land,' she
finished fiercely. 'I can't let him do that, no
matter. . .'

'No matter how much you love him,' the
Condessa finished drily for her. 'Shelley, I know
my son. . .I can't believe what you've told me is
true. Are you sure you're not just allowing yourself to be hurt unnecessarily by a vindictive
woman? Why don't you talk to Jaime about it?
Why. . .'

'No!' The denial was wrenched from her
throat. 'No. . .I can't. I felt all along that he
couldn't really love me; I should have listened
to my head and not to my heart.'

'Oh, Shelley.' The Condessa took Shelley's
hands in her own. 'My dear, how much of this
is my fault? I was so worried about the conven-
tions that I helped to push you into this marriage.
I knew you wanted to wait. What is it that really
frightens you? The thought that Jaime doesn't
love you? I assure you that he does. He's my
son, Shelley, and I know him very well, very
well indeed, and now I'm beginning to know you.
Ever since you and Jaime met you seem to have

been looking for some excuse to run away from him—and from yourself. Why? You've just told me you never really believed he could love you. Why not? You're a beautiful woman, inside as well as out, and my son has sufficient intelligence to see that. Are you sure the root of all this heart-ache isn't really your own sense of inferiority? I know what you had to endure as a child. I know how your grandmother treated you, but Jaime isn't your grandmother, Shelley; he's a man who loves you. . .'

The Condessa's words were too close to the truth to be borne. She had been subconsciously almost willing him to fail her; she knew that now. Because in some ways, now that he had done it was almost a relief. Now she needn't go on hoping any longer. Now she knew that he was just the same as everyone else, that her grandmother was right, that she was unworthy of being loved.

'He doesn't love me,' she protested bitterly. 'He loves Sofia.'

'You need time to think,' the Condessa told her. 'Yes, I know you want to see the *advogado*, but first we will go for a short drive together while you try and calm yourself. I always find it a most soothing remedy.'

Oddly enough, the Condessa was quite right. The stately progress of the chauffeur-driven Mercedes did have a calming effect on her over-wrought nerves, at least until she happened to glimpse a man in the street who from the back bore a remarkable resemblance to Jaime. She forgot that he had gone out this morning in a formal dark suit and this man was wearing one in pale grey, and jerked upright in the car, to stare almost hungrily out of the window. They passed the man and she looked back. he was nothing like Jaime, nothing at all.

To her surprise the car turned into an impressive modern hotel. 'We will stop here and have a cup of tea,' the Condesa announced, 'and then we will go back to the house and rest. This afternoon, if you still feel it is necessary, I shall make you an appointment to see the *advogado*, but I do advise you to talk to Jaime, Shelley.'

She wasn't going to be pushed into doing anything. Not now, but still she followed the Condessa into the plush foyer of the hotel, sinking almost ankle deep into a thick pile carpet.

'This way.'

The Condessa took Shelley's arm and led her into a richly decorated salon, already more than half full of elegantly dressed women, sipping cups of tea, while a girl played softly on a piano in one corner of the room.

This was obviously 'the' place to come, Shelley reflected, noticing the discreet display of jewellery and designer clothing. The décor was a little overpowering for her own tastes, especially in a modern hotel, but she could see nothing to criticise in the smiling welcome of the waitress who showed them to a table almost directly opposite the large open double doors that led back out to the foyer. Through them Shelley had an uninterrupted view of the reception area, busy now with a sudden influx of business-suited men, all apparently wanting attention at the same time.

The crowd cleared, their waitress brought them tea, and a selection of sandwiches and delicious-looking cream cakes, and while the Condessa poured for them both, Shelley's attention drifted back to the foyer.

Suddenly she stiffened as she saw Jaime walk up to the reception desk, and it *was* him, this time, there was no mistake about that. He leaned across to speak to the girl and she flashed a brilliant smile at him. Someone moved in front of him, blocking Shelley's view, and then when the stranger had moved away again Shelley felt her heart lodge painfully in her mouth. Sofia was standing beside Jaime, clutching his sleeve, and she was also taking the key the receptionist was handing over.

Shelley felt as though she was slowly being torn to death. She couldn't have dragged her appalled concentration away from the couple now walking arm in arm towards the lifts, to save her life.

The Condessa, noting her ashen face and fixed expression, touched her arm, and glanced over her shoulder, her curious, 'Shelley, what is it?' suddenly silenced as she too saw the other couple.

'Shelley, there must be an explanation,' she said quickly. 'It doesn't mean. . .'

'She gave them a key,' said Shelley tonelessly. She stood up jerkily, pushing the table and its dainty contents away so fiercely that she spilled the tea. Tears blinded her almost completely.

'I have to go,' she told the Condessa huskily, 'I'm sorry, but I can't stay. Not now. . .'

CHAPTER NINE

FORTUNATELY Shelley had kept the set of keys to the villa, which Jaime had given her. When they reached the *quinta*, she paid off the taxi driver, and although the staff were obviously surprised to see her back and alone, no one made any attempt to stop her as she packed her cases and loaded them into her car.

All the time she worked she was conscious of her fear that Jaime would follow her; that at any moment his car would draw up in front of the *quinta* and that he would try to stop her from leaving; that he would try to turn her own aching need for him against her and use it to overcome her will.

And it wouldn't be so very hard for him to do, not once he touched her. Admitting that to herself was the very worst form of torture. Despite what Sofia had told her, she still loved and wanted him. One rebellious corner of her mind wondered what she would have done if they had not been interrupted by his mother that night, and he had made love to her. Could she have turned her back on him so easily had there been a possibility that she might be carrying his child?

But he hadn't made love to her. Instead he had deliberately and intentionally aroused her to the point where she was incapable of thinking of anything other than his possession, using her unsatisfied desire for him to enslave her mind.

Once inside her car she forced herself to concentrate on her driving. The Condessa had almost persuaded her that perhaps she had been wrong, that perhaps she had been duped by Sofia after all, but seeing the two of them together like that, with Sofia clutching the damaging evidence of that key... No, that was something that could never be explained away.

Were they still together now, sleepily languorous after having indulged their appetite for one another? What would Jaime have said to her when he eventually returned to his mother's home? Would he have lied to her about some mythical business meeting, or would he simply have hidden himself away behind that icy silence she was becoming used to?

Even if he hadn't already guessed, he must surely know the truth by now. Sofia must have told him about their meeting and what had been said.

At first it had pleased her to pretend that Sofia's visit had simply been a social one; she had taken a painful pleasure in imagining him trying to work out exactly how much Sofia had told her, but now she bitterly regretted not flinging the truth at him while she had had the chance. And to think she had once thought him so moral, so upright!

A rush of tears almost blinded her eyes, and

she had to stop her car to wipe them away. She should never have come to Portugal. But if she hadn't she would never have learned the truth about her father's love for her. But nor would she have had to endure this agony of loving a man who had callously used her for his own purpose.

She paused in the action of re-starting the car, remembering what the Condessa had said to her. Honesty forced her to admit that there had been some truth in the older woman's words; she had been looking for an excuse to doubt Jaime's love, because subconsciously she had feared to trust him, dreading the shock and pain of ultimately finding that trust abused. But she had been right to mistrust his feelings for her, hadn't she?

She stopped again on her way to the villa, to buy herself some supplies.

Common sense told her that she should really have remained in Lisbon, but in her emotional reaction to seeing Jaime with Sofia, all she had wanted to do was to run away and hide, to put as much distance between them as possible, and the villa had beckoned to her like a shining light in unending darkness. Here, in the home that her father had willed to her, she would find sanctuary—or would she? What if Jaime came after her? Was he so desperate to obtain the villa and its lands that he would. . .?

What? Force her to hand them over to him? Hardly. She would have to write to the *advogado* now, instead of speaking to him in person. She

really was a fool for leaving Lisbon, but she had
been so emotionally overwrought she hadn't
stopped to think.

Would the Condessa tell Jaime what had happened? Stop thinking about him, Shelley warned
herself. If she could have scourged him from her
heart and her memory she would have done so,
but it was impossible. She still loved him. God,
how she hated to admit it, even to herself. What
had happened to her fabled remoteness, her
ability to protect herself from any sort of pain?
Both had deserted her the moment she met him,
or so it seemed with hindsight.

Part of her knew that, much as she would
loathe herself for doing so, if he were to come
to her now, to touch her, she couldn't guarantee
that she would be able to resist. Oh, she would
hate him for doing it, and hate herself as well,
but her hatred wasn't a strong enough weapon to
defeat her love.

She reached the villa just as the colour of the
sky heralded the onset of dusk. The traumas of
the day had resulted in an exhaustion that left her
body numbed but her brain overactive. She went
right through each room checking windows and
doors, and all of them were safely locked. Even
if Jaime did come after her he wouldn't be able
to get in. For the first time in her life Shelley
found herself wishing for the panacea of a
sleeping pill.

A hot bath and a milky drink were the best
substitutes she could find, but as she lay under

the soothing heat of the water, she acknowledged that her body was refusing to relax.

Every time she closed her eyes she was tormented by a confusing jumble of memories. Of Jaime, touching her as she had done that night in her bedroom, of Sofia, her eyes glittering with malice and relish. Of the Condessa, suddenly older and in pain, and then of Jaime again, and the way he had looked at her body, of the way he had seemed to want her, and yet all the time had not. And that was the greatest betrayal of all: that he should have deceived her in such a cruel way.

It was gone eight o'clock, too early to go to bed really, but she was so weary that was all she wanted to do. She was half-way between the bathroom and her bedroom, her damp body wrapped loosely in a towel, when she thought she heard the sound of a car outside.

Instantly terror invaded her body and she tensed, waiting to hear a peal on the outer doorbell. Instead as she listened, scarcely daring to breathe, she seemed to be surrounded by a thick muffling silence. . .

No matter how much she strained her ears, nothing penetrated the stillness, and in an agony of apprehension she ran to her bedroom and battled to unlock and open the heavy shutters.

Once she had them open she stared out into the front courtyard. Nothing seemed to move, but the moon was obscured by clouds and everything was cloaked in a thick, heavy darkness.

From the village the sound of a dog barking was carried to her on the breeze. She could smell the scent of the pines and realised that there must have been a recent shower to release such a pungent scent. As she stood by the window, rigid with tension, she waited, ears stretched to catch the elusive sound that had initially disturbed her, but nothing moved. Either mechanical or human.

Sighing faintly, she stepped back from the balcony and into her bedroom, closing the shutters behind her.

She was letting her imagination play tricks on her. Jaime wouldn't come after her; it was absurd to think that he might. A man who would marry a woman simply for financial gain was above all else a realist; he had to be, and as such Jaime was bound to see the pointlessness of trying to change her mind.

In her anxiety to check up on the car she thought she had heard, she hadn't bothered to switch on her bedroom light. An oblong beam of illumination from the half-opened door of the bathroom lit up the landing, her damp footprints clearly marked on the polished wooden floor.

As she stepped towards the door, remembering that she had left her night things in the bathroom, a shadow suddenly fell across the lighted doorway.

A scream rose in her throat, trapped there by a paralysing mixture of fear and shock. A filled the doorway, blotting out the light.

'Jaime!'

His name left her lips on a breathy, terrified whisper. Her body started to tremble like that of someone gripped in the most terrible fever. Without being aware of having done so, she took a step backwards, and then another one, her hands coiled tightly at her sides.

For one moment she could almost have believed he possessed some supernatural powers that had enabled him to suddenly materialise here in her doorway, blocking her only means of escape, she realised, as her heart lodged achingly in her throat.

As her initial shock receded and sanity reasserted itself, she heard herself saying almost stupidly,

'How did you get in? What do you want?'

As he lifted his hand she heard the jangle of keys, and cursed her own stupidity. Of course. . . of course Jaime would have a spare set of keys. All that idiocy of hers in locking all the doors and the shutters had been just so much wasted time. Where she had thought herself safe behind her locked doors, in reality all Jaime had had to do was simply to walk in. It was an omen she didn't want to take to its logical conclusion.

'What do I want?'

Surprisingly she saw that he looked unbelievably, furiously angry, a tight white line of rage drawn sharply round his mouth.

'Just what the hell is going on, Shelley?'

He dared to ask *her* that? Anger flashed in her eyes, and she saw from the brief darkening of his own that he had registered it. She had expected him to come after her, of course, but not so quickly, and certainly not in this white heat of rage.

'How. . .?'

'My mother paged me,' he told her curtly, anticipating her question before she could ask it. 'Something that had you any sense you might have thought to do. She was very shocked and distressed, Shelley.'

'And do you think I wasn't?' The words were out before she could stop them, an anguished lament for her lost dreams, but Jaime didn't seem to hear the agony in her voice.

'Going by the way you've been behaving these last few days, why the hell should you?'

'And that, I suppose, is why you went to Sofia,' said Shelley sarcastically, thinking that she could anticipate where the conversation was heading. 'Nice try, Jaime, but it won't work. I know the truth.'

'Like hell you do!' The words seemed to explode from his throat, 'And the reason I went to see Sofia was to try and find out exactly what it was she had said to my wife to turn her from a loving, happy bride into a cold block of ice. And now I know. . .*That's* why I went to Lisbon in the first place. I'm not a complete fool, Shelley; I knew Sofia had to have said something to upset you, and if you weren't going to tell me about it then she was. That was what I was doing in that hotel with her.'

'And for that you needed a private room,' she countered bitterly.

She watched Jaime's mouth compress and felt a tiny frisson of fear start up inside her. This wasn't going the way she had expected at all. She had anticipated contrition, coaxing, apologies and excuses, not this raging, barely controlled anger that seemed to burn up the air between them.

'Sofia's father just happens to own that hotel. She has a suite there; she lives there, Shelley. Now, you and I are going to sit down and talk.'

She didn't want to talk to him, she didn't want to hear anything that might weaken her defences even further. All right, so he was angry, and his anger made his explanations plausible, but how could she trust him; how could she trust anything he said?

Again, almost as though he had read her mind he said harshly, 'If you had trusted me in the first place none of this need have happened, but you don't, do you? You won't let yourself trust anyone. Well, that's your loss. I can't force you to give me your trust, but I can force you to sit down and listen to what I'm going to tell you.'

'I don't want to hear whatever it is you have to say, Jaime.' She turned her back on him and stared unseeingly at the half-closed shutters, hoping that he would read the determination in her stance and leave. If he didn't. . .nervously she contemplated the practicality of escaping via her balcony, reluctantly dismissing it as unfeasible.

Even as a child she had never had a head for heights, and the balcony was two storeys up. To jump from it was to invite death, and even to escape from Jaime she wasn't prepared to go to those lengths.

'Maybe not, but listen to it you will.'

He had himself under control now, his voice icy cold, or at least it seemed so, until he burst out furiously, 'Have you any idea what you've put me through this last week? Shelley, why the hell didn't you tell me what Sofia had said?'

'That she was your mistress? That you married me because you wanted the villa and its lands? And if I had told you, what would have happened? You would have denied it, and I. . .' She shook her head, unable to go on.

Shockingly, the ice was gone from Jaime's voice now, and she could hear the bitter rage reverberating through every harsh word as he said hoarsely, 'How dare you do this to me, Shelley? How dare you listen to and believe Sofia's lies? Love is a two-way thing, surely? Do you really have so little belief in me. . .so little trust that you think I would betray either you or your father like that—the woman I love—a man I have looked up to and revered for as long as I've known him? Is that really how you see me? If so, it's no wonder you were so reluctant to marry me. I thought we had something precious and rare, something we could build a future on. I thought I understood the reasons for your hesitancy, but I was wrong wasn't I? I didn't know you at all. You didn't want to love me, did you? You resented it, just as you resented me, so much so that you leapt at the first excuse to start mistrusting me!'

His attack had the advantage of surprise. Whatever she had expected, it was not this. Protestations perhaps, but protestations allied to soft words, coaxing caresses, pleas that she try to understand. He was right: she did not know him. This raging, furious anger was something quite different, something that she felt totally unable to contend with, something which, impossibly, seemed to spring from some deep well of pain and anguish.

These were the words of a man very deeply in love with a woman who had hurt him almost beyond bearing. The truth came home to her, and she could only stare at him in wild-eyed shock.

'Have you any idea what you've done?' he demanded in a husky voice. 'Less than a week ago in church you and I exchanged certain vows that tie us together for life, Shelley—I knew you were uncertain—hesitant, frightened even, but if I had known that you were capable of misjudging me like this. . .' He drew in a deep breath, his face oddly hollow and gaunt. 'A woman who cannot trust me is not my idea of a woman I can love.' He moved towards her and the light from the bathroom fell sharply across his face, revealing its taut bone structure and the dark flush of colour burning into his skin.

He looked like a man perilously close to the

end of his self-control, a man capable of whatever violence he felt necessary for the release of his feelings, and inwardly Shelley shivered, appalled by what she had done.

Now, when it was too late, she wondered how she could ever have been so stupid as to put any credence on what Sofia had told her. Even if she couldn't believe that Jaime loved her, she had known surely that he did love and venerate her father. She could see now that she had dealt his pride a blow that would demand payment.

Her eyes fell before the bitterness in his, and in a husky voice she said slowly, 'I couldn't bear thinking that you didn't want me, that you. . .'

He made a sound in his throat, the thick feral sound of a hunting animal intent on his prey.

Suddenly she felt cold, her skin chilled and still damp beneath her towel.

'Oh, I want you all right—even if I may not want to—and that isn't the only thing you were wrong about,' he added bitterly. He moved again, coming closer towards her, and panic flared through her veins as she saw the expression in his eyes.

His anger seemed to have burned away the outer veneer of civilisation, leaving only the inner, primitive man. She had never seen him like this, nor expected to. He was looking at her with a mingling of hunger and rage that made her shiver tensely. He was dangerous, menacing almost, a man violently close to the edge of control.

'I never intended to sell the villa to Sofia's father,' he told her bitingly, 'and if you'd stayed long enough to face me yourself, instead of running away like a little coward, I could have told you so. Sofia lied to you, Shelley.'

'She showed me the contract.' Stubbornly she tried to vindicate herself. 'Your signature was on it.'

'My signature was on a contract that relates to a completely different business deal I have with her father. You may remember I did mention it to you.' Now his voice was ice, cutting through her arguments with ruthless intensity. 'Did you read this contract?'

Angrily Shelley shook her head. 'How could I? It was in Portuguese.'

'Exactly.'

Triumph covered the ice in silk, and through the darkness she was acutely conscious of the tense rise and fall of his chest. Beneath the sophisticated covering of his clothes, he was as primitively male as the predator she had likened him to earlier, and just as dangerous. More so because, unlike the jungle animal, Jaime could think and reason.

Fear panicked her into silence, and her mind was wrestling furiously with what he had said.

The full enormity of what she had done yawned sickeningly in front of her, and just for a second her eyes met his in acute vulnerability. Quickly she veiled them, hiding her expression from him, clinging on to logic and reality. Hadn't

she, after all, known it might come to this? That
he might seek to confuse and beguile her into
believing him; that he might storm her senses
and force her to abandon both logic and reason?

But she hadn't thought to see him do so with
words. Rather, she had expected his attack to
be a sensually physical one, an appeal to her
vulnerable heart and weak desire for him.

Desperately she tried to retain her balance,
summoning everything she had to help her maintain her front of indifference. 'If what you say is
true, then Sofia lied to me. Is that what you're
saying? Why should she lie, Jaime?'

She saw the look that crossed his face, and
shuddered slightly. 'Because she hates me,' he
told her evenly. 'Sofia once wanted me not just
as her lover, but also as her husband. As I have
told you before, we have rather a strict code of
morals in this part of the world. Sofia has made
herself notorious with her numerous lovers and
affairs. Where once she was happy to shock the
conventional, now she wants their acceptance.'

'And by marrying you she could gain that
acceptance.'

'Yes. Sofia tricked you, Shelley. She tricked
you as easily as she might have taken sweets
from a child. I could have brought Senhor
Armandes here with me tonight. I could have
asked him to translate this so-called contract to
you. I could have asked him to confirm that it
was at my suggestion that your father left you
the villa—but what would be the point? You

made your choice a week ago. You preferred not to believe that I might be innocent. . .that there might be some explanation other than the one Sofia gave you. And why? Because you wanted to believe her. You wanted an excuse to run from me.'

Deep down inside herself, Shelley felt a burgeoning sense of horror. There was a kernel of truth in what Jaime was saying. And now, horribly, she could see how unfair and prejudiced she had been. She wanted to cry out to him that he didn't understand. That her vulnerability had come from her own lack of faith in her ability to attract him, from her own insecurity, her fear that he could not really love her and that one day, when it was too late, he would discover this for himself.

She wanted to tell him, but as she looked into his face and saw the bitter anger there, she couldn't find the words.

'What happened, Shelley? Did you wake up that morning and discover that you didn't want to marry me after all? That I might be acceptable to you as a lover, but that you didn't want to take the risk of marriage, of being my wife?'

As she looked up at him, Shelley felt as though something magical had died, and that, moreover, she had killed it herself. It was no good trying to tell Jaime the truth. If he had loved her, she had killed that love with her lack of faith and her thoughtless cruelty.

If their positions had been reversed how would

she have felt? Betrayed, totally and utterly.

'I should have known right from the start that something like this would happen, but it's not every day that a man finds the human embodiment of all his private fantasies walking into his life. It's apt to have a powerfully destructive effect on one's logic. And you *were* the embodiment of all my fantasies, Shelley.'

He turned his head and she saw the hectic colour staining his skin. In the half light his eyes glittered febrilely, his body gripped by a fierce tension.

'You've driven me half out of my mind, made me feel and want things I never knew myself capable of experiencing, but I was living in a fantasy world, wasn't I? The woman I loved simply didn't exist. I suppose I should have known. No woman of your race and lifestyle could remain virginal unless she was emotionally frigid. I dare say I'm not the first man whose life you've destroyed.'

Listening to him, Shelley was filled with a sense of desolation and waste. All too clearly now she could see that Sofia had been lying; using and manipulating her. No wonder Jaime was so furiously, so bitterly angry with her. It was no good trying to talk to him. He didn't want to listen. All she could do was wait until his rage burned out. She wanted to apologise, to protest that her guilt was one of loving him too much, not too little, but she knew that he wouldn't listen. How could she explain the years with her grandmother, the sense of inadequacy that had motivated her? How could she tell him that she had run from him in fear—fear of ultimately losing him? That she had chosen to shut herself off from the pain of that loss sooner rather than later?

His taunt about her emotional frigidity hurt, as he had meant it to, but she knew it wasn't true. She only had to look at him to go weak with longing, to ache to reach out to him.

She moved backwards, turning her head away, so that he wouldn't see what she was feeling, and as though somehow her movement infuriated him he reached towards her, his voice thick with bitterness.

'Don't turn away from me, damn you!'

His hands gripped her arms, and she tensed automatically before struggling to break free. That it was Jaime who held her was forgotten in the age-old fear of woman held prisoner in the arms of a dangerously angry man. As she struggled Jaime closed the distance between them, forcefully subduing her. One last desperate movement of her body brought it into harsh contact with his. As his hands moved to constrain her she felt the protection of her towel start to slide away from her.

Up until that moment she had forgotten her state of undress, but now, dismayingly, she was abruptly aware of it. She dared not move. Only the pressure of Jaime's body against hers, the painful grip of his hand on her waist held the towel in place. If he let her go. . .if he moved. . .

Her mouth dry with tension she fought to control the panicky thudding of her heart.

'It's all right. I'm not going to touch you.'

There was bitterness as well as rejection in his voice, and Shelley knew overwhelmingly that he meant what he said. 'I don't want a woman I have to take by force, Shelley, whatever you might think.'

What she was thinking was that beneath her towel, her body was suddenly frighteningly aware of him. In those seconds during which he had sought to subdue her, she had been reminded unbearably of the night in her bedroom, and her senses, ignoring totally the purpose of his touch against her now, had responded to those memories with shocking force. If she closed her eyes she could all too easily picture the breadth of his chest, smell the scent of his skin, taste the aroused salt texture of it on her mouth.

It had taken this. . .this catalyst of pain and anger to reveal to her the true intensity of her own feelings for him, to make her acknowledge that where there was love and desire such as she felt for him, there was no room for pride or fear. Shockingly, even now, when she knew that she had killed anything he might feel for her, she still wanted him. Still ached and ached for him.

She felt him move away from her, his hand leaving her waist, his body heat replaced by the cool night air. Her eyelids lifted, her senses helplessly in the grip of her physical desire. Without knowing she did so, she took a step towards him, the towel falling in soft folds around her feet.

Somewhere in the darkness of the room, she heard an agonisingly harsh breath drawn into tortured lungs and didn't know if it was Jaime's or her own. She tried to move, her feet tangling in the folds of her towel, her voice shaking with need as she cried out Jaime's name.

He caught her as she fell, his hands careful only to touch lightly on her skin, his arms rigidly outstretched to keep her off his body. Even so, her breath leapt in her throat, her body wantonly overthrowing the control of her mind and listening instead to the eager yearnings of her heart.

'Make love to me, Jaime.'

Even as the words trembled from her lips she couldn't believe she had uttered them. Neither, apparently, could Jaime. She could feel the tension emanating from him, feel it in the suddenly increased pressure of his fingers against her skin, but he made no attempt to draw her closer, nor gave any acknowledgement of her whispered request.

Desperation made her bold, and she pulled away from his constraining fingers and pressed herself against his body before he could stop her. She felt him shudder—once, and then his body went completely still.

'What the hell is this, Shelley?'

He sounded angry, and her heart dropped. Suddenly she felt chilled and foolish. What on earth had she expected? That he would be overwhelmed by desire for her?

Ashamed of her own wantonness, she pulled away from him, shocked by the sudden pressure of his arms as they fastened round her.

'Oh, no, you don't!' Now his voice was thick and husky, his expression hidden from her. He moved, and she felt the unmistakable surge of his arousal against her.

'What did you expect?' His raw words betrayed his knowledge of her shock. 'I'm a man, Shelley, and this time you've pushed me too far.'

He bent his head and her protest was lost beneath the fierce pressure of his mouth. He had kissed her before, but never like this, never with this hot raging need that bruised her lips, forcing them to part to admit the thrusting pressure of his tongue.

Locked against his body, Shelley felt herself shudder. A thousand reasons why she shouldn't be here with him like this seethed in her brain, but her body wilfully refused to acknowledge them; her arms reached up and locked round his neck, and when Jaime lifted his mouth from hers to stare down at her with blank, shuttered eyes she pressed herself eagerly against him, pleading for him not to leave her.

'What is it? Does rejecting me turn you on, Shelley, is that it? Does it make you eager for my lovemaking?' His hands roamed her body, burning trails of fire against her skin, blocking out the bitterness of what he was saying, making her so fluidly responsive to him that they didn't even matter.

'I want you, Jaime.' She whispered the words against his mouth, interspersing them with kisses, teasing its hard shuttered lines with the tip of her tongue. 'And you want me too,' she murmured when her teasing tongue could elicit no response. She started to move her hand down his body, and felt him clench all the muscles in mute protest. But there was nothing he could do about his physical arousal, and when she touched him she felt a small flare of triumph at the sensation of his hard, hot flesh beneath her fingertips.

'You asked for this—you know that, don't you?' The rough anger in his voice should have frightened her. Instead, as he picked her up and carried her over to her bed, all she felt was a fierce thrill of excitement. 'God knows I ought to resist.' He said it like a man driven to the edge of his control and beyond it, and despite the darkness, Shelley knew that as he stripped off his clothes he was looking at her.

The sound he smothered against her throat as he came down beside her sounded more like a curse than an admission of desire. But there was desire in the way his hands roamed over her body and fierce need in the hunger of his mouth against her skin.

He wasn't gentle and tender as he had been at his mother's, and yet her body delighted in his urgency, her fingers clenching eagerly into his hair as his mouth slid down over her skin to find the taut point of her breast.

The touch of his mouth sent feverish spasms

of delight exploding inside her, making her arch against him in frantic supplication. The increased pressure of his mouth, the almost painful scrape of his teeth against her tender flesh as he answered her mute demand, made her shudder with pleasure and moan his name.

His mouth left her breast, his chest contracting as he breathed in harshly. 'Is that what you like? Is it what you want, Shelley? Tell me how much you like it,' he muttered into her ear. 'Show me how much.'

His hands guided hers to his body, and she felt its tremor as she slid them against his flesh.

His skin burned against her palms, his eyes glittering strangely as he groaned deep in his throat. Mesmerised by her knowledge of his desire, Shelley pressed her lips softly to the hollow of his throat. She felt him tense, and then his hands were shaping her head, pressing her into his body, urging her mouth to move more intimately against his skin. She felt him shudder as she touched him with her tongue, her hands sliding down over his body to his hips. Suddenly shy and self-conscious, she touched him tentatively and then withdrew.

Almost instantly, his hand clamped down over hers, holding it against his skin.

'Do it, Shelley.' He sounded softly savage, his voice raggedly uneven. 'Touch me!'

Need swept away all her inhibitions, her hands untutored but eager in their discovery of him. When he moved away from her briefly Shelley watched him, worshipping him with her eyes, aching to reach out and touch him and yet making herself wait like a child with a long-desired store of favourite sweets.

His hand touched her, smoothing the sensitive skin of her thigh. Instinctively she reached up to tug him down towards her, drowning in the invasive heat of his kiss. His teeth tugged at her bottom lip, and she arched up against him, gasping in pleasure as she felt his hot skin caress her body.

The rage she had sensed in him before had been transformed into something else: a raw, elemental hunger that demanded satisfaction without any allowances for her inexperience, and yet there was no punishment in his touch, only a fierce and intense desire.

The stroke of his hand against the most intimate part of her released a flood of sensation, shot through with a need that made her press herself achingly against his touch, her mouth hot and trembling as she buried it against his throat.

She could feel the rigid muscles tensing beneath her tongue. His skin burned, the scent and feel of him filling her senses. Dimly she heard him moan. At first her name and then a rash of hoarse Portuguese that meant little to her. One hand caressed her, fuelling the ache that twisted and expanded deep inside her; the other tangled in her hair, trying to lift her mouth away from his body, but her hands had already found the hard contours of his hips and had felt the betraying shudder that wrenched through him.

His skin felt soft and smooth, like touching warm satin.

The need inside her escalated, and as he sensed her response to his caress, his fingers slowly and deliberately moved against her making her, heart pump and her breath catch in her throat in ragged gasps.

A sensation of eager, melting fluidity rushed through her, turning her muscles weak, making her eager to offer herself to him without restraint.

Of its own volition her body moved rhythmically against him, her hips arching, her breasts swelling with the same aching sensation that possessed her lower body.

Instinctively she sought the physical contact he was denying her, rubbing herself sinuously against his body, feeling her nipples peak at the soft abrasion of his chest hair.

A deep groan wrenched from deep in Jaime's throat, the fingers locked in her hair which had been trying to drag her head away from his body now urged her against him.

Shelley buried her face against his chest, breathing in the moist musky scent of him. She felt Jaime tug her hair and move against her so that her mouth pressed against the hard flatness of his nipple.

Tentatively she touched it with her tongue, thrilled by the sudden shudder of pleasure that racked him. Hesitantly she absorbed it into her mouth, caressing him the same way he had caressed her.

Almost instantly he stopped touching her. He didn't like what she was doing. Feeling sick at the abrupt cessation of his lovemaking, she made to move away, but he wouldn't let her. His hands locked round her head, his body arching against her mouth.

'Don't stop, Shelley, don't stop doing it.'

His fingers tangled in her hair, and then one hand slid down her arm to take hers and place it against the hard thrust of his body.

Touching him so intimately made her ache with longing, her body quivering with the same sensation his stroking fingers had aroused.

As though he knew what was running through her mind, Jaime pushed her down against the mattress, dragging her hands away from his body and pinioning her arms away from her own.

There was something achingly erotic about lying here like this, so acutely vulnerable to him. Part of her instinctively shrank from the bold intimacy of his scrutiny. Defensively she gripped her legs together and started to lift them so that she could protect herself from his appraisal, but he moved too fast for her, trapping her with the weight of his thigh. The rough hairiness of his leg rubbing against hers was an alien and yet an exciting sensation. Something inside her seemed to twist and melt and turn her insides to liquid. As though Jaime had experienced the sensation for himself, something possessive and very mas-culine gleamed in his eyes.

As he lowered himself over her body, the remnants of her virginal fear made her tremble and ask huskily, and, she reflected later, ridiculously, 'What are you going to do?'

Her eyes were open very wide, holding his as though her life depended on it. She could barely draw a breath without trembling, and now when the moment she had incited and deliberately aroused had arrived she shrank back from it.

'What am I going to do?' How deep and throaty his voice was. 'Well, first of all this.' His mouth touched one nipple and then the other, in the lightest of caresses. 'And then this.' He was still holding her arms away from her body, and she quivered as she felt his lips move against her skin, down over her rib cage, tasting the smooth flesh of her waist, and then lower so that his tongue brushed seductively over the slight swell of her stomach.

She was no longer afraid of him. Now she was afraid of herself and of the feelings he was arousing inside her. Wanton, erotic feelings that had nothing to do with the person she had always thought herself to be.

His hands freed her wrists, but she was too bemused to move her arms. His tongue circled the indentation in her belly, making her quiver with renewed sensation. A tense, coiling ache was building up inside her, an urgent heat burning through her veins.

She felt Jaime slide his hands down over her hips and then slip them beneath her, lifting her slightly. Her legs felt curiously weak, and opened easily as he nudged them apart with his knee. She felt his mouth against her inner thigh and tensed in shock, even though she had guessed what he meant to do.

Knowing didn't stop her from tensing against the shocking intrusion of his tongue touching her with an intimacy she had known existed but never dreamed of experiencing. She tried to drag herself free of his hands, frightened by the intensity of the sensation that shot through her. She didn't want to feel this awesome, unknown pleasure that touched her senses. She didn't want to be so vulnerable to anyone, least of all Jaime.

His tongue ceased its delicate exploration, and his mouth moved back to her thigh. She shuddered in relief, fighting to regain control of her reactions.

'What's wrong? Don't you like it?'

'Like it?'

'Or are you just frightened? Is that it, Shelley? There's nothing to be afraid of.'

His voice was soft, the words soothingly rhythmic, his mouth moving gently against her inner thigh.

Slowly she started to relax, only to tense up again as his mouth moved back to the centre of her body.

This time his touch wasn't tentative, but determinedly assured. Shelley reached out to push him away. 'No!'

Jaime raised his head slightly and looked at her. 'Yes, Shelley,' he contradicted flatly, and her stomach quivered as his breath moved against it. 'Yes...yes...yes...'

He kept on reinforcing his intentions until the sound was smothered against the intimacy of her, his mouth caressing her with an erotic heat that she fought to oppose until it was impossible any longer to hold back the flood tide of sensation convulsing her.

She neither knew or cared that she had stopped resisting him and that instead her body moved eagerly to the subtle instruction of his mouth. Her nails dug into his shoulders as she experienced for the first time the reality of feminine sexuality, and as the pleasure flared higher and higher and then finally receded, she no longer cared what emotions she exposed to Jaime.

Through a lethargic fog of pleasure she felt him slowly release her. He moved to lie beside her, and for the first time she realised that while she had reached a peak of sexual satisfaction, Jaime had not shared it with her.

A sense of failure enveloped her, the swift downward plunge of her emotions from high to low, bringing stinging tears to her eyes. Abruptly she turned away from him, curling into a tight little ball. His hand gripped her shoulder, and she felt the warmth of his breath against her ear.

'What is it?'

'You didn't really want me at all, did you?'

She couldn't keep the bitterness out of her voice. He had aroused her and satisfied her, but the knowledge that he himself neither wanted nor needed her completely wiped out all her own pleasure. By not wanting to possess her, he had robbed her of her femininity, made her feel that she was inadequate as a woman.

'What makes you say that?' His voice was dry, his fingers biting hard into her skin.

'I should have thought it was obvious.' She couldn't look at him, and her voice trailed away miserably.

'Shelley. . .'

'Don't lie to me, Jaime. You aroused *me*. You made love to *me*, but that's all it was, wasn't it?' She was suddenly terrifyingly, humiliatingly sure that she had hit on the truth. 'You don't want me in that way, you. . .'

The words were silenced in her throat as Jaime wrenched her round so that he could look at her. His mouth was hard with tension, his hands bruising her skin as he held her captive.

'Of course I want you, you little fool, but I didn't want to hurt you. I wanted to show you what pleasure there could be before I had to show you any pain. Of course I want you.' His voice was softer now, less harsh, his hand sliding into her hair.

'Then why don't you make love to me properly?'

She felt his tension and thought for a moment he was going to move away, his hand was still in her hair, angling her face so that he could look at her.

'Is that what you want?' His mouth touched

hers, and shockingly she tasted her own scent on it. 'Do you want me inside you, Shelley, is that what you want?'

The tip of his tongue caressed her lips, stroking softly over them in the same way that she had already imagined the silken caress of his flesh within her own.

Her mouth had gone dry, her heart pumping unevenly. 'Yes.' She mouthed the word against his lips. 'Yes, I want it very much.'

She felt him move, the weight of his thighs settling between her own. The heat of him was something she hadn't expected and she trembled.

'Still want me?'

His eyes searched hers, and Shelley wondered if he was remembering his vow. If he was it obviously didn't matter. Her own betrayal of him, her lack of trust had destroyed what had been between them. She was his wife and she loved him; wasn't that reason enough?

'Yes. . . Yes. . .I still want you. . .I want you now, Jaime. . . Jaime!'

She moved urgently against him, gasping as she felt the swift intrusive thrust of his body within her own. For the space of a heartbeat all sensation, all movement was totally suspended. Pain, sharp and blessedly brief, took away her breath. Within her she felt Jaime tense, but the pain was already fading and in its stead. . . Wantonly, joyously she arched up against him, and after his initial hesitation felt the assured controlled movement of him inside her.

'Is it what you wanted? Do you like it?'

If his movements were controlled, his voice wasn't, and to hear the rasped words falling against her skin filled her with a pagan delight— and a need to seduce his body, until it mirrored the hunger she could hear in his voice.

'More, Jaime,' she begged against his throat. 'More. I want all of you inside me.'

It was as though she had invoked some magic spell. His hands gripped her hips, teaching them the rhythm of his body, his mouth hot against her skin as his control splintered and she experienced for the first time the driving intensity of a man's desire.

Her body, already sensitive to his touch, already aware of the pleasure he could give it, responded eagerly, absorbing the hard heat of him, travelling with him to a peak of pleasure that brought her name from his throat on a guttural cry of triumph.

She was reluctant to let him go, curling tiredly into his arms, wanting to beg him to understand that it had all been a mistake, that she had been guilty perhaps of loving him too much rather than too little, but somehow, as she tried to form the words, they slid away from her.

CHAPTER TEN

SHELLEY woke up slowly, her body aware of the changes that had taken place within it before her mind properly assimilated them. Last night she and Jaime had made love with a passion she hadn't known existed. She had gone to sleep in his arms, but now she was alone.

Apprehension drove out her waking euphoria. She sat up, reaching instinctively for the sheet, as the bedroom door opened.

Jaime came in, carrying a mug of coffee. His mouth tightened as he looked at her, and Shelley knew she had been right to feel apprehensive.

'I'm sorry about last night.'

His clipped voice wasn't that of the lover who had whispered in the darkness how much he desired her and how much she pleased him; his eyes avoided contact with hers as he deliberately looked away from her.

'It won't happen again, Shelley. It wouldn't have happened last night if. . .'

'If I hadn't begged you to make love to me,' she said quietly. Pride was the only thing that was holding her together now. She had killed Jaime's love, and she had deserved to lose it. How ironic it was that her pain was caused by her lack of trust instead of an excess of it.

'I would like you to come back to the *quinta* with me this morning,' he went on, making no comment on her remarks. 'There are things that have to be sorted out before. . .before I can set you free.'

Had his hand trembled as he set the mug down, or had she simply imagined it? If she reached out and touched him now, would he respond to her as he had done last night? Perhaps, but it wasn't merely his sexual responsiveness to her that she wanted. She wanted what she had so recklessly thrown away. She wanted his love. . .his belief in her. . .his trust.

Suddenly his words struck her like blows. Set free? What did he mean?

'I was wrong to rush you into marriage; I can see that now. I should have waited. . .taught you to trust me first. I'd underestimated how much damage your grandmother had done, and overestimated your. . .your feelings for me.'

'But last night. . .'

'Last night both of us reacted out of character; both of us needed the release of what happened between us, but good sex isn't any basis for marriage, at least not for the sort of marriage I want,' he said harshly.

'But we can't divorce.'

Shelley managed to whisper the words past the tight lump obstructing her throat.

'No, I'm afraid that's not possible. I was thinking more of a legal separation. When I came here last night I had intended to discuss having our marriage annulled, but. . .'

But she had destroyed any chance of that. Numbly Shelley stared at him. What he was so calmly discussing with her was no more than she herself had decided upon not twenty-four hours before, and yet now, she knew it was not what she wanted. What she wanted was this man and what they had shared last night—what they could have shared right from the start of their marriage if only she had had the courage to trust him. Yes, she could admit that now. Trusting him would not have been the weakness she had always perceived it to be; it would have taken an act of courage, an act of faith. But she had lacked both, and because of it, she was now being punished. Dear God, how ironic it was! Sofia had achieved her wish after all. She had destroyed their marriage.

She couldn't let it end like this. There must be some way. Wildly she searched for a means of turning back the clock, of blotting out the reality of what was happening.

'Jaime, what if we. . .if there would be a child?'

A mask seemed to come down over his face, blanking off all expression. 'I wouldn't wish on any child of mine the misery that permeated my own childhood. Quarrelling parents is a cross no child should have to bear. You will always have my financial support, of course. . .whether there is a child or not.'

He sounded as though they were discussing a piece of furniture. She wanted to cry out to him that she loved him; that she wanted *him*, but she couldn't. What right did she have to claim that now? Would he believe her? Would he even care? This morning all the passion and fire she had known last night were gone. He was as remote and unreachable as a statue.

'It will take some time to make the arrangements. In the meantime I suggest we return to the *quinta* and continue to live there as before. My mother. . .I shall ask her to remain in Lisbon until everything is finalised. She will be disappointed.'

'How long. . .' Shelley licked her dry lips as she saw the glitter of something—anger? pain?—burn in his eyes.

'No longer than necessary,' he told her harshly.

'Jaime—'

'No, I don't want to talk about it, Shelley. I wronged you, not once but twice. I dragged you into my personal fantasy—something I had no right to do.'

'And now that you know I'm not the girl my father painted, you don't want me any more; is that it?'

She threw the words at him in her pain, but he didn't make any response, simply walking out of the room and closing the door quietly behind him.

*   *   *

If Shelley had thought the first week of their marriage agony, during the second she began to learn what that word really meant. Jaime was a cool, distant stranger she didn't even dare to talk to. He spent most of his time in his study, and didn't even eat with her any more. She was alternately torn with a desire to go to him and plead with him to change his mind, and an equally intense need to escape. Living like this was tearing her apart. It was worse, far worse than the pain caused by her jealousy of Sofia, because this time her wounds were self-inflicted.

Towards the end of the week Jaime told her that the *advogado* was coming to the *quinta*.

'I shall discuss with him how matters can best be arranged. He will be here late this afternoon. Unfortunately I have a meeting with the wine-growers' association which I must attend. Perhaps I could ask you to make him welcome in my absence?'

He wanted *her* to welcome the man who was going to send her away from him? She wanted to scream at him that he was asking too much, but instead, she merely gave him a blank smile. Pain was something she was getting used to; she barely felt his sharpness any more, only its unending agony.

Senhor Armandes arrived at four o'clock. Shelley offered him refreshment, and was aware of the concern in his eyes as he looked at her. She must hardly look the picture of a blooming bride. Had he any idea why Jaime had sent for him? What did it matter? He would know soon enough, but first there was some business of her own she wished to accomplish.

If the *advogado* was surprised by her request that she wished to transfer the deeds of the villa and its surrounding land to Jaime, he didn't betray it, commenting only that he was glad that at least some small part of the coastline would be preserved from such speculative ventures as that undertaken by various Lisbon builders.

The mention of Sofia's father made Shelley frown. 'My father was totally against the land being sold for such developments, I know.'

'Your father, and Jaime also. Both of them were dedicated to preserving the land as it has always been. I know that your father planned to plant vines there as Jaime has done at the *quinta*, but he died before he could put his plans into operation. Of course it was his intention that the villa and its land would be returned to Jaime on his death, but Jaime suggested that he should leave it to you.'

How ironic that the lawyer should tell her this, now when it was too late, but the blame was all hers. Sofia could never have made trouble if she had only had the courage to believe Jaime when he said he loved her. And now it was too late.

The *advogado* seemed to see nothing odd in her wish to sign over the villa to Jaime. The papers would take some time to prepare, he warned her, but they should be ready by the end of the week. It was plain to Shelley from his conversation that he believed Jaime had sent for him to discuss some matters concerning the *quinta* and his purchase of some outlying land. Shelley did not disabuse him. She left him an hour before dinner.

When Jaime returned Shelley left the two men together.

Upstairs in her room she prepared for dinner, first washing her hair, and then sitting down in front of her bedroom mirror to dry it.

In the mirror she saw the bedroom door open and Jaime walk in. Immediately she switched off her hairdryer. Her heart was thumping unsteadily, and she was glad that the thick towelling of her robe concealed its betraying thud from him.

He was frowning, and she noticed with a pang that the grooves alongside his mouth had deepened, and that his face looked faintly gaunt, as though he had lost weight.

'What's all this about you wanting to sign the villa over to me? I have just come from Senhor Armandes and he has told me of your wishes.'

She had to turn away from him so that he wouldn't see the pain in her eyes. 'It's for the best, Jaime. . .a clean break.'

'You mean so that you have nothing to remind you of me. . .of our marriage,' he said with a savagery that shocked through her. 'And if you do carry my child. . .will you dispose of that as well?'

The cruelty of it made her cry out in protest, her eyes filling with the weak tears she had tried to conceal. 'How can you say that? You are the one who is sending me away. You are the one who. . .'

He turned towards her, a driven expression on his face.

'No. . .no, don't touch me.' She retreated from him instinctively, knowing if he touched her she would start begging him to let her stay. 'If you do, I'll never be able to leave.'

The admission was wrenched from her against her will, her body shaking with nerves, Why on earth hadn't she asked Senhor Armandes to say nothing of her intentions regarding the villa? Of course Jaime wouldn't want her to give it to him; he would want nothing of hers now, not her love, not. . .

She heard him breathe in raggedly, her eyes drawn to his face. He looked like a man at the very edge of his self-control.

'Do you honestly think what you've just said is an incentive to stop me?' he ground out incredulously. 'Dear God, Shelley. . .' He saw the look in her eyes, his mouth twisting cynically. 'Don't look at me like that. Not unless you. . .'

He wanted her. He still wanted her! She could see it in his eyes, feel it in the tension invading the space between their bodies. As her eyes widened in recognition of his desire, he made a thick bitter sound in his throat. 'Shelley, Shelley, what are you doing to me?'

He reached for her almost clumsily, kissing her like a starving man. Her body seemed to melt into his and become part of it. She moaned his name beneath the famished heat of his kiss, winding her arms round his neck.

'Jaime. . . Jaime. . .please don't send me away. I know I hurt you. . . I. . .'

He released her so abruptly she almost fell over.

'Send you away?' He stared at her. 'What the hell are you talking about? I'm not sending you away, I'm giving you your freedom.'

'I don't want it. I want to stay here with you. . . be your wife. . .' She could see him tensing every muscle as though in rejection of her soft-voiced plea.

'Don't say that unless you mean it.' His voice was harsh with pain. 'I can't face a second rejection from you, Shelley; I think it would kill me.'

She started to cry then, not for herself but for him, for the pain she had caused him.

He made a sound in his throat like a man tortured to the point of death and then hauled her back into his arms, holding her so tightly that she could feel the fierce, almost frantic thud of his heart.

'You said we had to part,' she sobbed. 'I thought it was because you didn't love me any more. . .because I'd let you down with my lack of trust.'

'No. . .no! I was sending you away because I thought it was what *you* wanted. You'd begged me not to rush you into marriage, but I wouldn't listen. I had to have you. I was terrified when you said you wanted to go back to London. I'd wanted you for so long, and then to think that I might lose you—I didn't plan for my mother to interrupt us that night, but when she did. . .I wasn't altogether sorry because I knew she would insist on us marrying. I thought once we were married I could convince you that I loved you, but instead. . .'

'Instead I listened to a vengeful, jealous woman.'

'I'd have given my life not to hurt you like that. . .I knew Sofia must have done or said something, but you put me off the scent when you told me that you weren't sure of your feelings for me. I decided the only way I could be sure was to force Sofia to tell me the truth.'

'And did she?'

'She was going to. I made it clear to her that where she was concerned there were no lengths I wasn't prepared to go to get the truth out of her, but my mother paged me before Sofia started to talk, and she told me instead.'

'I thought I'd hurt you so much by not having faith in you that I'd killed your love.'

Jaime took her hands in his and lifted them to his mouth palms upwards, dropping soft kisses into their cupped centres.

'Nothing could do that,' he told her quietly, 'no power on this earth or outside it.'

'But you were still sending me away.'

'I thought it was what you wanted.'

'Even after we'd made love?'

He took a deep breath that told her of what he was feeling. 'I never doubted that physically you wanted me. I was afraid that you would resent me for that as well. I wanted to give you a chance to discover just what you did feel for me, without the confusion of sexual desire.'

'And now you know that I do love you.'

'Now that I know that, there's no way I'm ever going to let you go.'

His hands slid beneath her robe as his mouth moved passionately against hers. Shelley forgot that she was supposed to be getting ready for dinner; she forgot that Senhor Armandes was probably already waiting downstairs for them, and it was Jaime who had to remind her unsteadily half an hour later that they were already late.

It must have been one of the shortest meals on record, Shelley thought a little guiltily two hours later as she walked into her bedroom, but this time not alone. Jaime was behind her, closing the door, switching off the light, taking her into his arms with an urgency that left her in no doubt of his feelings for her.

'Poor Senhor Armandes,' murmured Shelley against his mouth. 'To come all this way for nothing. He's bound to think it rather odd. Especially you saying that you wanted an early night because you have to be up early in the morning.'

'What's odd about that?' He was kissing her throat, teasing the pulse that beat frantically there, his hand sliding down the zip of her dress.

'Jaime, it's barely ten o'clock!' Shelley protested.

'Mmm...as late as that? We'd better stop wasting time then, hadn't we?'

His mouth silenced any indignant protest she might have been about to make, and her body trembled eagerly in his arms as he slid away her dress.

'I should have known the night we made love that you loved me,' he said softly as he picked her up and carried her over to the bed. 'There is more than one way of giving trust, Shelley. You gave me yours when you gave me yourself.'

His words wiped away her last feelings of guilt, her love for him shining in her eyes as he placed her gently on the bed, quickly stripping off his own clothes before joining her.

Now no words were necessary; the way they touched and came together said it all, but as though he wanted to banish her doubts for ever, as he made love to her Jaime told her again and again of his love, so that it filled her senses like the softest, clearest light after the misery of the intense darkness. He loved her and she loved him. What possible need had she for anything more?